To Mr. IJ

From
Emily

2002/2003

Twelve
Christmas Stories
by
North Carolina Writers
and Twelve Poems, Too

edited by Ruth Moose
Illustrations by Talmadge Moose

DOWN HOME PRESS, ASHEBORO, N.C.

ISBN 1-878086-61-8

Library of Congress Catalog Card Number
97-069662

Printed in the United States of America

Book design by Beth Glover
Art by Talmadge Moose

Down Home Press
P.O. Box 4126
Asheboro, N.C. 27204

Dedication

For my father,
Ardie Lloyd Morris,
who had a Christmas heart
all year long.

Acknowledgements

The editor wishes to acknowledge the following publications in which these materials were previously published:

"Advent" was first published in *Kentucky Poetry Review*.

"Angels" appeared originally in *Mrs. Houdini* from University Presses of Florida.

"Christmas Night" appeared in *A Walk Into April* published by St. Andrews Press.

"Christmas with Dylan" originally appeared as "Thumbin' in the Wind" in the Christmas l985 edition of Raleigh's *Spectator Magazine*, where permission to reprint the piece here is gratefully acknowledged.

"Ellen Foster's Christmas" is excerpted from the novel, *Ellen Foster*, published by Algonquin Press of Chapel Hill.

"Firecrackers at Christmas" appeared originally in *At the Edge of Orchard Country* published by Wesleyan University Press.

"In Lieu of Mistletoe" is reprinted with permission from the author and originally appeared in *Redbook*.

"Home for Christmas" is excerpted from the book *Only When They're Little* published by Appalachian Consortium Press.

"Martha and the Three Magi" was first published in 1972 in *The Longview Journal*.

"Rich in Spirit" is reprinted with permission from the author and originally appeared in *Redbook*.

"Yule Log" is reprinted by permission of *The Hudson Review*.

Thanks also to Nancy Joyner, Margaret O'Connor, Rebecca Rust, Alice Cotten and the NCWN.

Contents

Twelve
Christmas
Stories
by
North Carolina
Writers

and Twelve Poems, Too

Lost and Found

Sue Ellen Bridgers

Christmas Day is the one time in the year Daddy's family gathers. They used to come to Grandmother's house but she's not well enough to have all that fuss and bother in her house, even with family bringing most of the food, so now they come to us. They all live close enough to drive over for the day. Counting the children, that's twenty people and every year Mama spends days figuring out how in the world she's going to get them all to the table at the same time. We always end up bringing folding tables from church and covering them with cloths that hang too long on the sides but have to overlap in the middle because they're too short the other way.

Mama frets and complains because this is not as nice as she'd have it but she's glad

11

to be responsible all the same. Mama loves the attention of it—you know, everybody saying what a marvel she is and how does she ever get it all done and why, Philip certainly knew what he was doing when he "discovered" her. The great-aunts and uncles love to think about that. It seems romantic to them because everyone of them married somebody they'd known all their lives and don't have anything exciting to tell about it.

"Philip and Dottie did different now," Uncle Willard says practically every Christmas, reminding us that in addition to Daddy finding Mama at a meeting, Aunt Dot met Uncle Gerard on the train to New Orleans which is even more exotic and almost as good as a shipboard romance. Nobody in Daddy's family has ever been a seafarer except Uncle Willard himself, who sailed to Europe on the Normandy when it was temporarily turned into a troop ship during World War II. He still remembers the crystal chandeliers in the dining room and the heavy wood paneling so polished it glowed. He always tells about Aunt Dot and Uncle Gerard on the train just like he was there, and then goes on into his story about the Normandy. We have heard it a million times.

I am the oldest of the first cousins. Aunt Dot and Uncle Gerard have four children, two girls and two boys. One too many, Uncle Gerard says, to fit nicely in the back seat of the car. All the time, he's eyeing them like he's deciding which one to dispose of. Mama is so offended by this. Every year she says, "Well, just give any one of them to me because they are equally precious."

The kids don't pay any attention, not to Uncle Gerard or to Mama. They are loud and happy and positive about everything. The boys run outside with Buddy no matter how cold it is and play football with anybody who happens by. They don't seem to mind they've had to leave their big presents at home.

Aunt Dot's little girls bring their new dolls with blankets and bottles and clothes in little plastic carry-alls and make a house at the top of the stairs where they can see and hear everything but be in their own make-believe world at the same time. They want me to come see how they've set up their houses but don't want me to watch them play. I remember how that was—still wanting to pretend but a little embarrassed by it.

This year everything is the same except naturally we are all older. The grown-ups sit at the table after dinner and I stay with them. It is already late afternoon so the boys dash outside one more time, saving dessert until later when it's dark and they're too tired to do anything but watch television and stuff their faces again.

Mama is in the kitchen waiting for the giant percolator to quit perking and searching for the coconut cake. Great-aunt Virginia always brings a coconut cake for Christmas although, according to Mama's down-east customs, ambrosia is a more appropriate dessert. Aunt Virginia's coconut cake is highly regarded, though. It's four white layers with mounds of fluffy white icing you can only make if the weather is dry. Aunt Virginia turns up her nose at the frozen variety of coconut and grates a fresh one herself after heating it in the oven to get the shell loose. She puts some of the coconut milk in the batter to make it even more special but even when the cake is perfect, Aunt Virginia can find something wrong with it. Her little criticisms and her family's praises go back and forth all the time we're eating it, like a ticking metronome.

But today Mama can't find it. She knows Aunt Virginia brought it. Didn't everybody go through the usual oohs and aahs? Didn't Aunt Virginia lift the edges of the plastic wrap to let a little air in? But where in heaven's name is it?

The kitchen is crowded. There are stacked dishes, half-empty bowls and casseroles, melting congealed salads, a turkey carcass sticking up out of the roaster, a half-carved ham still gleaming with sugar and pineapple, baking sheets with cold Parker House rolls stuck to them. Every surface is covered so Mama has no choice but to look in the cabinets, the oven, the packed refrigerator, even goes out into the laundry room. The washer and dryer are covered with coats but she actually looks in the dryer! She goes back into the dining room to look at the sideboard once more, just like a gigantic four-layer cake could be overlooked the first time. Our sideboard is small and it's covered with dessert plates and cups and saucers and the pies—pecan, pumpkin and apple—because although the coconut cake is the showpiece of Haskett desserts, it isn't enough to feed us all.

I can see Mama is really worried. She's

standing in the kitchen, patting her foot like she's nervous but with her fists pressing on her hips like she's also defiant about something.

"What is it?" I ask her in the doorway. I'd just as soon not actually enter the kitchen. Once you're in there, you're trapped into some kind of duty, maybe even washing the china which is much too fragile to go in the dishwasher.

"I can't find Aunt Virginia's cake," she hisses between her teeth.

"Well, where did she put it?" I whisper back.

They are getting restless behind us. The table is cleared and now there are just the cranberry sauce and gravy stains, sprinkles of pepper, the unused cream and sugar to look at. Wax is beginning to drip over the rims of the candlesticks and the nandina berries in the centerpiece are dropping one by one in the heat. The relatives are tired, too, and the tree lights from the living room seem blurry, like the whole afternoon is suddenly dazed. The men want to head for the living room where they'll pretend to watch television but mostly doze and the women are thinking about getting at that mess in the kitchen. They're impatient to beat each other to a particular task, like they each have a clean-up skill the others aren't practiced in.

"I don't know where she put it," Mama mouths. "If I knew, I wouldn't be standing here." She is so upset. Beads of perspiration sparkle across her forehead and her mouth is grim.

"Well, just ask her," I say and Mama gives me an exasperated look, as if doing that is so obviously the last resort. "I'll ask her," I say and go right ahead and do it.

"Why, I don't know!" Aunt Virginia cries. "Didn't I give it right to you, Liz?" she calls into the kitchen.

"No, Ma'am," Mama says back in a fakey sing-song voice, as unperturbed as she can make it.

"Well, it's got to be somewhere," Aunt Isabel says. "It didn't just grow legs and walk off, did it?" Aunt Isabel has never been lavish in her praise of her sister-in-law's coconut cake but now, potentially deprived of it, she is concerned.

"Lordy, let me think a minute," Aunt Virginia says, clutching her wadded napkin to her bosom and giving us an embarrassed smile. "I came right through here with it. I remember that because you were standing right there in the living room, weren't you, Dot? And we couldn't even hug because of it."

"That's right," Aunt Dot says.

"Well, where did I go with it then?" Aunt Virginia wants to know.

"I went to help Uncle Willard out of his overcoat," Dot says.

"She did," Uncle Willard remembers. "She went to help me so she doesn't know a thing in the world about that cake, Virginia," like he's got to defend Aunt Dot or something.

"I saw it," Uncle Fred says. He is Grandaddy's widowed brother and he never says anything worth hearing that I can tell. Now seeing the cake is all he remembers about it.

"Well, my goodness," Aunt Virginia cries. She is truly upset now. "I have never in my life had a cake disappear like this!"

"It hasn't disappeared," Daddy says. "It's just temporarily misplaced."

"But where?" Mama wants to know. She's getting mad now. I can tell she's thinking the men ought to stay out of it. None of them seems likely to find a cake.

"Well, we'll just have the pies right now," Daddy says, not seeing what danger he's in. "The cake is bound to turn up."

"Well, I for one won't rest until it's found," Aunt Virginia says. "That cake was a lot of trouble to make."

"A cake can't just be here one minute and not the next," Grandmother says, as if that clears up the whole matter.

"Have you looked everywhere?" Aunt Isabel asks Mama, which is a mistake if I ever heard one.

"Well, I haven't gone upstairs," Mama says. There's no avoiding her frustration now. It's a spectacle of bright cheeks and mouth twitches and they all see it and one by one I see it dawning in their faces that she's really not one of them. She's from down-east, for heaven's sake, and she can't find a cake in her own house. What in the world was their Philip thinking?

"I know it's not upstairs," Aunt Virginia says. "One of my cakes has never been upstairs."

Daddy laughs. I see it coming on his face and there's no stopping it. I smile, too, caught like I am in the doorway between Mama and Daddy. I'm a mix of the two of them. Anybody will tell you that.

"Maybe the boys know where it is," Uncle Willard says, newly inspired. He likes a good mystery.

"I doubt that," Aunt Dot says, "but I don't suppose it'll hurt to ask." She starts up.

"No, I'll go," Uncle Willard says. "A little stretch of the legs will do me good." He scrapes back from the table and totters up.

He is halfway across the living room when Aunt Virginia says, "Willard, what in the world is that on your pants?"

We all look. There's a white rim on one side of his gray suit trousers. Mama tries to beat me to his chair but I get there first so I'm the one that lifts it up, a coconut cake flattened to a couple of inches under its plastic wrap. The shape of Uncle Willard's bony bottom is right there, perfectly indented in Aunt Virginia's hard-to-make frosting.

"I declare, Willard," she says. "You've been sitting on it!"

"I have not," Uncle Willard answers, still intent on asking the boys.

"Well, just look here then," Aunt Isabel

says, pointing to the cake. "What does that look like to you?"

Uncle Willard turns back in slow motion, like he's leaning on a cane we can't see. "Confound-it-all," he says, looking at the mashed cake but not at us. "I thought I had a mighty soft seat."

They laugh, even Aunt Virginia. Even Mama. Somebody says we ought to save the cake to show it to the boys. The little girls come see and they beg to have a piece, no matter how it looks. They like things gooey and all mixed together.

Aunt Dot lets them. "After all, what harm can it do, covered up with plastic like it is," she says.

There is stone silence at the table. I can hear the percolator in the kitchen and then Buddy shouting at one of the cousins outside, "Throw me the damn ball!"

For once, it's a blessing they're all hard of hearing or else they are too busy concentrating on the ruined cake I'm still holding. They watch Aunt Dot peel off the wrap and start spooning lumps of cake into the bowls Mama's holding out for her.

"Well, in that case," Aunt Isabel says, "I

believe I'll have a little taste."

Aunt Dot and Mama are holding on to their giggles so tight they both look like they're about to die. Eventually I guess we all eat some. It is considerably better than you might think.

There is a light snow falling when Daddy's family starts for home.

"Doesn't look like it's going to amount to much," Uncle Todd says.

"Never does anymore, not like when I was a boy," says Uncle Fred.

"Well, there was that one in '55," Uncle Willard says. "Remember that one, Virginia?" He is blocking the way out the front door and they all stand behind him in their coats and hats and mufflers waiting to go.

"Not now, Willard," Aunt Virginia says. "We'll talk about it next time."

"Let's just get going," Grandmother says to Isabel and Todd. "I want you to drive slow, too. I'm not about to get killed on the way home."

They go out under the porch light, most of them stooped a little under the weight of their heavy clothing, holding on to each other and then to the railing at the steps. Daddy goes ahead of them, brushing the light snow off the walk with Mama's outdoor broom.

"Merry Christmas!" they suddenly call back to us on the porch. It's like one voice coming out of the dark. Mama's got her arm across Buddy's chest like she can keep him from bolting out into the snow and Aunt Dot is holding her littlest one who in turn is holding a doll that cries and wets and does I don't know what all.

"Wonderful dinner, Liz!" they call with quavery, cold-struck voices. "The best I can remember!"

They are acknowledging Mama and she shivers under the porch light. She is grateful it's over but proud, too, to have served and survived Daddy's family.

"Well, that's done," she says finally when they are all in their cars and making a procession down the street to the stop sign, their signal lights blinking to show they intend to turn in different directions, going home.

We're standing here in the quiet watching Daddy come back up the walk with the broom over his shoulder. There's a dusting of snow on his sweater and in his dark hair. Now Aunt Dot leans toward Mama and with her free hand takes Mama's. I have never seen them touch before except the hugs that accompany comings and goings.

Behind us is the warm, lighted house still smelling of roasted turkey and coffee and sweet desserts. It's cold and we aren't dressed for outside but suddenly I want to be out there with Daddy looking back at them so I dart off the porch and grab his arm, slowing him down so we both can see Mama and Aunt Dot under the light. They are still holding their youngest. They are holding hands, too, and they look tired and happy and peaceful all at once.

Yule Log

Michael McFee

Just before Christmas, every year,
dad's rich friend Winston would send one
packed in dry ice, in a special box
stamped *Biltmore Dairy* in dark green cursive.

We'd bear it to the kitchen counter
and juggle the smoking ice into the sink
and slowly unroll the frozen paper
around this first and sweetest of presents:

a yule log made of *Premium* ice cream.
Its chocolate rind looked exactly like bark,
down to the scattered nut-knots;
its pith was a plug of creamy butter pecan

so authentic it almost had rings.
Mom held the long knife under the spigot

until it was finally hot enough
for Dad to slice a piece for each of us,

a thin section from this section
of the tree of endless good cheer and luck
and wealth enjoyed at the Estate.
But we weren't jealous, there in the kitchen

of our home built of skinny logs
on land owned long ago by George Vanderbilt;
as dry-ice fog tried to sneak
cheap melodrama into the scene we simply
stood on the verge of Christmas
then filled our empty spoons and lifted them
and burned that log in our mouths,
its cold fire falling, filling our aching chests.

Martha and the Three Magi

Irene Cheshire

"When Mama and Mary Elizabeth get inside Woolworth's, there's no getting them out!" Aunt Ellen declared. She was speaking of my grandmother and me. I was nine at the time.

Aunt Ellen's husband owned a grocery store and they had carpet even on their sleeping porch floor.

On past Christmases, she bought without our choosing (or paying for) the few presents that Grandmother and I gave to our friends. She said that it was foolish to drive fifteen miles from Tusleeta to the old home-place, drive back to Tusleeta, then "—waste what is left of my day while those two dilly-dally for hours in the dime store!"

This was a special Christmas. It was the first one that our friend, Willie Jack, would spend in the County Home. Willie Jack, who was fourteen, could not walk because Sheriff Robert E. L. "Pistol Pete" Debar had shot him. Sheriff Debar said it was Willie Jack's father he was aiming at, and that he was sorry about Willie Jack, but nobody believed him. Willie Jack's father left the county, and in the fall, when his mother died of influenza, he was taken to the County Home for he had no other kin.

"Positively NO!" Aunt Ellen said when we pleaded to take Willie Jack in. "I am putting my foot down!"

Aunt Ellen was very good at putting her foot down.

Sometimes my grandmother would declare: "If we were independently wealthy, things would be different!"

My father, who traveled with a Chautauqua, often forgot to send money, and Grandfather was a timber cruiser and did not come home often.

It was only two weeks until Christmas. We were determined that *this* Christmas we would choose and buy a present for Willie Jack and take it to the County Home ourselves. (We had saved our birthday money for this very purpose.)

Merely *asking* Aunt Ellen to take us shopping would not work.

"We must make our plea in the Christmas spirit," my grandmother said, "and set it down in print on the prettiest cards we own!"

The only picture cards we had were the treasured few that our Atlanta relatives had sent us.

Early one December morning, with my two cats, Queen Mary and Colleen Moore watching from the sunny window sill, we sat at the kitchen table where it was cozy and warm, and cut pictures from our small hoard. After pasting the pictures onto penny postal cards, we wrote a message to Aunt Ellen on each one.

On the different cards we wrote: *It is more Blessed to Give than to Receive*, and, *Our Lord Loves a Cheerful Giver*. On one we wrote: *Take Heed of the Need of the Widow and Orphan*. Later Grandmother said she was ashamed that we sent that one. It wasn't really true, except about Willie Jack being an orphan, and besides she had made it up, because she couldn't recall off-hand the Scripture reference to widows and orphans.

On the fifth card we wrote: *Not Frankincense and Myrrh, but a gift chosen by our own hands do we desire to give our Friend, Willie Jack, spending his first Christmas in the County Home without friend or kin. P.S. We will be expecting you. We have already decided what to buy. Your Loving Mother and Devoted Niece.*

The mailbox was a mile down Watermelon Road and in front of the house where Willie Jack had lived. All the windows were broken, and from beneath the porch a thin grey cat, who I did not know, peeped at us. Near the crumbling chimney the wind shifted dry leaves and whispered: "Willie Jack—Willie Jack." Thinking of my lost friend was like hearing trains crying in the night as they search for a lighted place to stop. I held tightly to my grandmother's hand as we walked back down Watermelon Road.

Three days before Christmas, Aunt Ellen came to take us shopping. Our present to Willie Jack was to be a shaving set in a splendid red and gold genuine simulated leather box, that we had seen in Woolworth's when we visited Aunt Ellen in the early Fall.

"It will probably smell to High Heaven, and Willie Jack doesn't have a whisker on his face," Aunt Ellen said, as we got into her car. But our minds were made up.

Uptown in Tusleeta, my aunt said, "Since you know what you're going to get, I'll let you out in front of Woolworth's, circle the block, then pick you up."

I looked with dismay at my grandmother, who made a "Shhhing" movement with her lips. "You had better park," she said, "We could change our minds, you know."

"Oh, Lord, here goes my day!" Aunt Ellen moaned, and found a parking place close to Woolworth's.

Woolworth's was not a place to run into while someone circled the block. Woolworth's was a palace in London. . .a carousel of bright lights spilling over beads and bracelets. . .a place where the smell of popcorn and candy and perfume met you at the door, and goldfish swam in crystal bowls. Where beautiful girls with Maybelline on their eyelashes like ladies in the picture show stood behind tinkling cash registers. In my nine-year-old heart I was sure that the finest thing in life would be to stand behind a Woolworth's counter when

I became old enough.

After we bought the shaving set from a lady who made us laugh when she asked was it for my husband, Grandmother went to the back of the store so I could buy her presents. I bought a little glass swan filled with perfume and a bottle of Hinds Honey and Almond Cream. (Sometimes Aunt Ellen said that Grandmother looked "country" and leathery.) I longed to buy her a lace handkerchief, but I had to save enough money to buy tuna fish for my cats, and a plug of Brown's Mule Chewing Tobacco for Sam, who could not speak or hear, and who lived in a small gray cabin between our house and the mule lot.

It was late when we got home and Grandmother went inside to light the kerosene lamps and start supper. There was still enough light for me to see Sam making his way down the lane. Sam helped with Grandmother's garden and kept her woodbox filled.

With my cats meowing and rubbing against my ankles, I waited on the porch so I could show him the present we had bought for Willie Jack. It was drizzling and Sam had slipped a white bathing cap, discarded by my aunt, over his head and was wearing his old overcoat that covered him from his chin to the tops of his worn brogans.

Sam had round surprised eyes and a sad squeezed face. Rheumatism caused him to walk with a sort of rocking chair shuffle. As he rested on the wooden porch bench, I showed him the shaving set. He pointed in the direction of Willie Jack's house.

"Yes, it's for Willie Jack," I said, facing him and speaking slowly. I pointed in the direction of the County Home. "We will take it to Willie Jack on Christmas Day."

Sam's eyes grew rounder and he pulled the collar of his overcoat closer about his chin.

Before Willie Jack was taken to the County Home, Sam had visited him each day. That past spring he had given Willie Jack a yellow biddy that Willie Jack named "Henny Penny." When Henny Penny got big, Sam carved a willow whistle so Willie Jack could call her to his side. She would jump onto the bed and eat corn that Willie Jack sprinkled on the counterpane.

"Lord pity Willie Jack's poor mother cleaning up after that chicken," Aunt Ellen said when we told her of Henny Penny.

33

On that bad day when Sheriff Debar took Willie Jack to the Home, Sam with Henny Penny clutched in his arms, had stood in the lane with his eyes on the road until dark set in.

We did not see Sam at all the next two days, and thought he must be spending some time with Rosella, his married daughter, who lived a half mile down Watermelon Road.

Christmas morning finally came. Grandmother started a fire in the range to warm the kitchen and we opened our presents. We saved the ones that we had bought for each other until last.

The little glass swan was even more beautiful than I remembered. Grandmother placed her on top of the pie-safe opposite the window in a sparkle of sunlight.

As Grandmother rubbed the Hinds Honey and Almond Cream on her face and hands, she said, "Well, your aunt can't say that I look country and leathery anymore—why, I'm going to use this cream every single day from now on!"

My presents from Grandmother were a string of ruby beads beautiful enough for a princess, and a box of peanut brittle.

"Mary Elizabeth," she said as she adjusted the beads around my neck, "If we were independently wealthy, these would be real rubies!"

We were to eat Christmas dinner with Aunt Ellen, but Grandmother had waited until Christmas morning to bake teacakes for Willie Jack. "I couldn't bear a house on Christmas Day without the smell of some cooking going on," she said. She put raisins and cinnamon in the teacakes. When they finished baking, I spaced them, except for two, in a box and tied a red ribbon around it.

Grandmother spread the table with her lace cloth and we each had a teacake with coffee. Because it was Christmas, we used our celebrating cups—the ones with the golden rims that my great-great-grandmother brought over from England. Although my coffee was mostly milk, it made my cup, which was as thin as a butterfly's wings against the sun, even prettier.

Aunt Ellen said that it was foolish to "celebrate" with "priceless cups in a run-down farmhouse."

"Life is moments, not tomorrows," my grandmother had replied, standing tall as a queen.

We were ready to go when we heard Aunt Ellen's car in the lane, and hurried out so we wouldn't keep her waiting. I carried the shaving set that we had tied with red ribbon, and Grandmother carried the box of teacakes.

As we reached the car, Sam shuffled around the corner of the house. He hugged a grocery sack close to his chest, and his overcoat flapped at his ankles. He looked at the car, at my grandmother, then down at the sack that he held tightly. Grandmother reached for the sack, but he moved away, then came closer to the car.

Aunt Ellen drummed her fingers on the steering wheel.

"Sam wants to go with us," Grandmother said. "He has a gift for Willie Jack."

"Oh, Lord!" my aunt said. "Sam can't speak a word nor hear one, and *you* say he wants to go to the County Home and take a gift to Willie Jack! Well, thank the Lord it's not raining, or he would be wearing that darn white bathing cap for everyone to see!"

She pointed to the back seat of the car. "Get in, Sam," she said.

Sam did not move, except to shift his round eyes from his plain brown sack to our bright packages.

"Wait," Grandmother said. "He wants a ribbon for his sack."

"Oh, Lord!" my aunt groaned.

Grandmother hurried into the house, then came out with a ribbon for Sam's sack. As she tied the ribbon, he held the sack so she couldn't see what was inside.

Finally we got away from the house, with Grandmother and me squeezed up front with Aunt Ellen and Sam in the back seat.

"Sam didn't get his present at Mr. Beasley's store," I said as we rode toward the County Home. "It's in a sack from the foundry commissary in Slaghill."

I thought of Sam's trudging the three miles down Watermelon Road, to the banks of the Black Warrior River, and I was puzzled as to how he had managed to get someone to put him across to the Slaghill Road.

To cross the river, first you must stand at the landing, and shout: "Ho! The Ferry!" When Thurman (who ran the ferry) heard you, he would jump into a skiff (if you were on foot), and row to the landing. If you were on a wagon

37

or a car, he brought over the cable-pulled ferry raft.

That day as Thurman was pulling my aunt's car across the water, he told us that Sam had waved a pine-limb—"until he caught my eye—no tellin' how long the pore feller had been standing there!"

The County Home was a gray, unpainted wooden building huddled in a flat dirt yard. Although the sun shone brightly that Christmas morning, the scene was bleak and cold. I felt cold, too, as I thought of Willie Jack, who loved the outdoors, being inside such a dreary place.

Aunt Ellen parked near the narrow plank steps in front, and Grandmother said, "You don't have to go in with us."

"Thanks!" my aunt replied.

She watched as the three of us, each with a ribboned present, got out of the car. My grandmother always looked real lady-like and walked erectly, but I wished that I could have given her some new shoes for Christmas. Although I had used lots of black polish on her Sunday ones the night before, they looked worn. My ruby beads sparkled but I had shot up during the summer and my last winter's coat was shorter than my dress. Sam's overcoat was so worn that he looked as if he were molting.

Aunt Ellen was a city lady and I wondered if maybe she was ashamed of us.

Inside the County Home, there was a smell of cabbage and disinfectant, and the floors were grease-spotted. Willie Jack's mother had cleaned her kitchen floor by scouring it white with sand, each Saturday morning.

A big red-faced lady stepped forward and told us where Willie Jack's room was.

"You wait 'til they come out," she said to Sam.

Grandmother calmly looked at her. "He's with us. Come, Sam."

The lady muttered to herself, sniffed, and went on her way. My grandmother could be very imperious when it was necessary.

To reach Willie Jack's bed, we had to walk past beds with real old men in them. Their eyes were so sad and hungry that for a moment, I wanted to run back to the car.

Willie Jack caught sight of us. He tried to raise his arms, then fell back against a lumpy pillow, and breathed in short gasps.

39

"I've missed you-all," he paused to catch his breath, "Ever' minute of ever' day." He looked at Sam. "I still got the willow whistle you whittled me—"

Willie Jack had no strength in his arms and I was close to tears as I opened the package that held the shaving set.

"Gosh!" he said, closing his eyes and sniffing deeply. "Gosh, it smells better'n that honeysuckle down by the spring branch!"

Sam shuffled close to the bed. He handed his grocery sack to Willie Jack slowly and carefully as if there was a present more precious than the crown jewels inside. Willie Jack couldn't untie the ribbons so Sam worked them loose. As he leaned over the bed, his overcoat touched the floor. His round eyes swept from sack to Willie Jack's face as he displayed what was inside the sack.

"Sam! Oh, Sam!" Willie Jack cried, as his tears spilled onto the present. "I bet nobody in this whole world ever got two whole coconuts for Christmas—except me!"

"Well, are you Three Kings of the Orient ready to go home, now?" Aunt Ellen asked as we climbed into her car.

"Yes," my grandmother replied. "If our good Martha is ready to take us there. I was always partial to Martha," she added.

"Thank you, Mama," my aunt replied. Her eyes were shiny bright like the Christmas star. "I wish, though, that someone would teach us Marthas how to tie red ribbons around our packages." She sighed, "Even Sam—limited as he is—knows the importance of red ribbons!"

Only after Grandmother read to me, the story of Jesus visiting the home of Mary and Martha did I understand what my Aunt Ellen meant about the importance of red ribbons.

A Christmas Night

Sam Ragan

It was a cold night
And there was ice on the road,
Our car started to slide
As it moved up the small hill,
And the headlights caught the old man
In a thin jacket
Pushing a cart filled with sticks.
There were some bundles and a package
Piled on top, and the old man
Grinned and waved at us
As he pushed the cart
Into the yard of the little house
Where a single light shone.
The tires gripped the road
And we drove on into the darkness,
But suddenly it was warm.

The
Loving-Hands-at-Home
Nativity

Shirley Cochrane

It was Christmas, 1935, and we were not
spending it in my beloved house—spacious,
comfortable if slightly shabby, light-filled, and
looking out on magnificent woods. We had
had to rent it out for three-hundred dollars a
month (a princely sum in those days) and
lease a cottage for thirty dollars. This move
helped us survive the Great Depression, during which my grandmother's tea room and
candy shop folded and my mother's salary at
the University of North Carolina (Chapel Hill)
was cut. With my mother, grandmother, and
great-grandmother, all widows, I hunkered
down in our modest quarters and waited for
better times.

Would that I could describe myself as a
noble, self-sacrificing child, a healthier ver-

sion of Little Nell, but honesty forces me to admit that I whined a good bit. I had lost my cozy little room with the bay window and view of tree tops and now had to share a bedroom with my great-grandmother and the cat, both of whom snored. And there were other grievances.

This Christmas, my mother explained, I could not have the bicycle I'd asked for, and as for the nativity scene—well, we would just have to see. What I wanted were those beautifully carved-in-Germany figures—Mary, Joseph, and baby Jesus, with animals and wise men and angels—the whole magnificent and expensive set.

Christmas morning I woke to rich smells coming from the kitchen and a blazing fire in the fireplace—creations of my early-rising grandmother. And there was the nativity scene. One of our porch stools—the kind with wooden logs for legs and a splint bottom—had been upended and a slanted cardboard roof erected on top. A star rose at the back, and I recognized its brilliance as coming from the gold paper my grandmother had used for wrapping her chocolate candies when she was still in business.

I also detected thimbles and spools, junk jewelry and tinfoil, and swatches of velvet, silk, and satin, as well as pieces of worn fur and cotton batting—lots of cotton batting. Cotton for the wise men's beards, a whole flock of cotton sheep. The baby Jesus (a small celluloid doll lying in a matchbox with glued-on toothpicks to simulate wood) was wrapped in cotton swaddling clothes. Cotton angels with celluloid wings were suspended from the manger roof.

Pieces of my great-grandmother's discarded Persian lamb scarf had been used for Joseph's hair and beard and as trim for the kings' robes; also for the heavy coats of various cattle. One of these was a large bullock with bone hairpin horns standing guard at the back of the manger.

But Mary—there she was, a German-carved masterpiece, with blue and rose garments and a halo. My mother had managed to buy one figure. An odd mating—magnificent Mary beside a Joseph fashioned out of worn-out socks and scraps of Persian lamb. But I was charmed—as I am now, remembering the scene.

As years passed and our fortunes im-

47

proved, we returned to our roomy house. Even before that move I had received a splendid new blue bicycle. And all the figures worthy of the beautiful Mary were added to the nativity scene. But it is that first home-made one that hangs in my memory, outshining all later gifts.

In the Next Christmas

Jean Rodenbough

In this season of delight
Joy comes slowly
To those whose long night
Does not forget easily
The year passing in long stretches
Of absence or fear or other pain

This season of light comes again

But only when we remember
What has gone before
So that we understand the fragile gift
Of life in whatever form
And more blessed when we discover
Brief moments of life centered
In the Holy Presence

We wait for more

In Lieu of Mistletoe

Marianne Gingher

My parents married in Dallas less than two months after my mother had stood on her head. Valentine's Day, 1946. Then my father finished his medical residency, received his officer's commission from the Navy, and was shipped off to Guam in June. My mother had just learned that she was pregnant. She went back to Virginia to live with her parents until my father could make arrangements with the Navy for her to join him.

Six months later, on December 1, my mother boarded a DC-7 for San Francisco, the first leg of the long journey to Guam. She'd expected to feel delirious with excitement. For weeks she'd been packing her steamer trunk, dreaming of this reunion. Why, she'd threatened to row herself to Guam if the Navy didn't come through. Katharine Hepburn would have! But as her plane lifted her up and away from familiar ground, as she watched her hometown recede into the protective huddle of the Blue Ridge Mountains, she shivered. She was twenty-one years old, a wisp of a girl, headed to an island ten thousand miles away, to have a baby with a man she hardly knew.

"Where you headed, honey?" a woman sitting across the aisle asked her.

"Guam," she said. The word had always sounded exotic to her, like the hum of a tropical butterfly with wings as big and brightly colored as fans. But when she pronounced it for the woman on the plane, "Guam" sounded lonesome—like "gone."

"*Guam*?" The woman looked impressed. "You must really love him," she said.

Yes, she'd thought. Cochrane There was that: love. People in love committed themselves to risky adventures all the time, didn't they? She had only to think of the movies to feel reassured. Had anybody ever made a movie about a man and a woman in love who stayed safely put, gathering dust like knickknacks? What did it matter that she'd been separated from the man she loved for so long that she couldn't remember which of his cheeks dimpled when he smiled or on which side he parted his hair? When she stepped off the boat, in the full bloom of pregnancy, her hair cut shorter now, so what if he might not immediately recognize her? They'd been strangers once before, hadn't they? Lightning could strike twice in the same two hearts, couldn't it?

She arrived in San Francisco feeling downright heroic. No, thank you, she said to a man who offered assistance, she'd carry her *own* suitcase, she'd flag her *own* taxi.

She checked into her hotel room—her ship wasn't scheduled to leave until morning—and for a while she gazed out the window that overlooked the bay, feeling festive and inspired. Down below she saw street lamps twined with greenery, and Christmas shoppers hustling. She heard the sweet, melancholy ringing of Salvation Army bells.

She hadn't bought my father's Christmas present yet, and that afternoon she rode a cable car to shops the hotel clerk had recommended. She'd brought one-hundred dollars with her on the trip—it was all the money she had in the world—but when she saw the sterling silver cigarette case displayed in the jewelry shop window, she didn't think twice. She envisioned a canopied patio at the edge of the Guamanian jungle, moonlight, scents of trees frilly with blossoms, a man in a turban playing the violin. She imagined herself and my father seated together at a table, their heads inclined lovingly toward one another. My father took from his breast pocket (he was wearing a tuxedo) a shining cigarette case. Perhaps it was something she'd seen Humphrey Bogart or Claude Rains do in the movies. He flipped the case open, never taking his eyes from her own, removed two cigarettes, lit them simultaneously, and offered her one.

"Ninety-four dollars," the shopkeeper said. The price included monogramming.

Never mind that the ship's departure was delayed two days or that the Navy had temporarily lost her steamer trunk. Never mind that she lived on bouillon made with tap water in her hotel room because she'd spent all her money on his gift. She slept with the silver case beside her on her pillow. She gazed into its beautiful, shimmering surface as if into a crystal ball and conjured my father's face. She sent him a one-word cable from the hotel: "SOON."

The weather turned cold and rainy as the ship heaved across the Pacific for twenty-one days. My mother shared her cabin with two other seasick women, veteran Navy wives who described for her the champion-size centipedes on Guam, the overly sociable mice and spiders, the irrepressible rust and mildew.

"Did you know there aren't any bathtubs?" one of the women said. "Do you know what they bathe babies in? The surplus nose cones of B-29 bombers!"

The other woman shuffled a deck of cards, telling fortunes to pass the time. "Want to know yours?" she asked my mother.

"I already know everything that I need to know," my mother said dauntlessly. "I'm spending Christmas with the man I love."

"On *Guam*!" the fortune-teller said, as if hurling a curse. "No mistletoe, no Christmas tree, and not the faintest hope of snow. A typhoon, maybe!"

But early on December 24, when land was sighted, even the dour fortune-teller whooped and threw her cards into the air. On the ship's deck, a sailor brought out his harmonica and played "Jingle Bells," and a few passengers began to dance. Sunlight bloomed in the sky.

My mother leaned against the railing of the ship, waving to the crowd waiting on the dock. She felt as buoyant as a kite in her new maternity dress—"Pacific Ocean blue" was how she'd described it to him in a letter. And now, after weeks of weather as gray as doubt, the ocean, beneath blue sky, looked blue. Beyond the wharf the island—not flat like the lily pad she'd imagined, but hilly—rose lush and green.

"Do you see him?" the fortune-teller asked.

"Not yet," my mother said, shading her eyes, searching for a man with a dimple, a man who parted his hair on one side.

"Who did you tell me he looked like?"

"Ronald Colman."

"I've been at sea too long," the fortune-teller said. "They *all* look like Ronald Colman to me." Then she gave a little shout of recognition. "I found him! Yes, you're *right*! Oh my, what a doll!"

"*Where*?" my mother cried, standing on her tiptoes.

"Beside that jeep."

"I still don't see him."

Then the fortune-teller gave a yelp "Oh, dear," she said. "You should have let me read your cards." She grabbed my mother's arm and gave her a mournful look. "He's standing between two military police. It appears that he's been. . .arrested."

"But that's impossible!" my mother said, laughing. "That's simply out of the question."

"How well do you know this fella anyway?" the fortune-teller said.

Sure enough, as my mother descended the gangplank, my father, accompanied by two military policemen, strode to meet her. She was crying—tears of joy, tears of dread, she didn't know which—but she threw her arms around him and kissed him as completely as she'd ever kissed him in her life. The MPs looked down at their shoes, grinning. Then, apologetically, one of them said, "Okay, Doc, you've seen her. We'd better get a move on." Of course, she'd seen enough movies to know that in the midst of such an embrace he'd be collared and dragged off to jail.

"Right," my father said briskly, loosening his hold on her, his face sobering.

"Whatever you've done, I forgive you," she said bravely.

"There's been a plane crash," he said. "I've been asked to help. It's a rotten greeting, Janie, but I'm really needed."

She felt like a fool, riding along in the jeep beside him, listening to him tell the MPs that she'd thought he'd been arrested. The men's shoulders shook with laughter. The baby inside her kicked gleefully, as it found her mistake funny, too.

The plane had crashed on the far side of the island. The MPs, assigned to collect and transport all the medical personnel they could find, had intercepted my father on his way to the dock. He'd barely been allowed to meet her ship. She supposed she should feel grateful.

In minutes the jeep screeched to a halt beside a row of metal Quonset huts flanked by palm trees. "Please hurry, Doc," the driver said. My father helped my mother down from the jeep, then raced ahead of her into the middle hut. By the time she'd reached the door, he was hurrying out again, his medical kit under his arm. He kissed her quickly, then ran toward the jeep, his stethoscope around his neck. "Good-bye!" she called, waving after him. "When will you be back?"

"Soon," he called, like an echo of her cable. Then her husband was gone—gone on Guam—and she was standing on the threshold of her new home, on Christmas Eve, alone.

Inside the Quonset hut, she plopped down in the only armchair and gazed around until her heart felt pinched and cold. What a stark shelter it was! He'd warned her in letters that it was essentially one room, meagerly furnished. She saw a two-burner stove and a squat refrigerator. The entire living area was gray: gray metal walls, gray upholstery on the sleeper sofa, a gray metal card table, gray venetian blinds. It was as if the drab weather of doubt that had beset her during the Pacific crossing had fronted onto the island and hovered over her still.

She marched to a window and snapped open the blinds; to her relief sunlight poured cheerfully in. It twinkled along the metal poles that stood like spindly columns, holding up the ceiling. Like *Christmas* trees, she thought—if one used her imagination.

She couldn't work fast enough to duplicate what she'd envisioned: a Christmas tree where there'd been no inkling of one before. She dug in her purse for nail scissors. In a cardboard box on top of the refrigerator, she located string, waxed paper and mucilage in a rubber-tipped bottle. She found a bundle of her love letters that he'd saved.

She paused only a second, then slipped off the twine that bound them and began to cut. She made a paper chain first. She cut out shapes of angels, bells, stars and snow-flakes. She worked all afternoon, decorating the pole. When she was finished, she wrapped up the sterling cigarette case in a square of waxed paper and propped it against the base of the pole.

The sky darkened; an amber moon swelled over the palm trees. She set the card table with the tin plates she'd found. She made coffee, opened tins of meat, arranged the meat on a platter with sliced pineapple. In another Quonset hut, she could hear children singing Christmas carols. She sank into the big gray armchair to wait, but my father didn't come home that night.

Early on Christmas Day she was awak-ened by an official-sounding rap on the door.

A young corpsman, delivering her steamer trunk, saluted her. "Any word about the plane crash?" she asked anxiously.

"No fatalities, but it's bad," he said. "The hospital's full up. They've set up tents at the crash site." He shook his head sadly. "It was a transport plane, men going home for Christmas. Need me to bring you anything, ma'am?" He had a Southern drawl, a face as pink as a country ham.

"Did you know anybody on the plane?"

"My best buddy," the corpsman said gravely. "He was going home to his wedding."

"Well, maybe he'll be all right."

"I'm praying," the corpsman said. He brightened with sudden recognition and pointed to the pole. "Hey! I really like your Christmas tree. That's the spirit!" Those were the only words of cheer she heard that whole long Christmas Day.

It was the morning of December 26 when my father finally slipped into bed beside her. He slept for fourteen hours. When he awoke, he pointed to the decorated pole and asked groggily, "What's that?"

"What do you think it is?" she said.

"I don't know," he said, still rubbing his

eyes.

"It's nothing then," she snapped. "Go back to sleep."

But he got up, showered, and went directly to the hospital. It became his routine: tending the plane-crash victims until he reached the point of complete exhaustion, then collapsing into the silence of deep, excluding sleep. She tried to lie close to him, but he was used to sprawling, to having a whole bed to himself. He thrashed his legs fitfully, pushing her out.

She could not keep up the spirit. On New Year's Eve, as he was preparing to go back to the hospital, she began to unwrap the metal-pole Christmas tree. She wadded up the love letter ornaments and threw them away. "What's happened?" she asked him. "You're always running away from me. I've tried to be brave, but I just can't stand it anymore."

He glanced at his watch. He was late. "This is my life, Janie. This is what I have to do."

"What about *our* life? I came halfway across the world to be with you. I'm pregnant with our child, and you haven't made a minute for me!"

"We're not urgent. We're not a life-or-death emergency. We've got the rest of our lives together, for better or worse," he said, his voice rising.

"I'm not staying if it gets any *worse*," she wept. "We missed our first Christmas together, and you don't care."

"I care," he said, tiredly now. "But forty-two injured men missed Christmas too, and I'm trying to see that they live to see the next one."

"What if I told you I'm leaving?" she cried.

"I'd say you weren't the girl I thought I married."

"Who wants to be her?" my mother said bitterly. "She was a fool."

She ran past him, out the door of the Quonset hut, sobbing. She was halfway to the beach when he roared past her in the jeep. Where the road forked, he turned toward the hospital.

The night sky with its blizzard of stars reminded her of winter. The beach gleamed in the moonlight, as if covered with snow—and the weather in her head felt like the dead of January. She imagined a newsreel—*Pregnant Wife Found Frozen on Tropical Island*—and she shivered.

She thought ruefully of the sterling silver cigarette case, which she'd never gotten to give him. *Had she ever even seen him smoke?* It occurred to her that much of what she thought she knew of him was her own invention. Wasn't it possible that the same rhapsodic imagination that bought cigarette cases and concocted metal-pole Christmas trees had made up a husband too?

She was so absorbed in these thoughts that she lost track of time, and when two warm hands slipped over her shoulders she jumped.

"It's me," my father said.

My mother started to cry.

"I have a terrible confession," he said, turning her to him. "I wouldn't be here if some guardian angel at the hospital hadn't taken a good look at me and sent me straight home."

My mother wiped her tears and gazed stoically out to sea. "How far away is China?" she said.

"You were ready to swim for it, weren't you? You were just going to take right off."

"I thought it might be worth a try," my mother said.

"I saw in the trash can that you'd ripped

up all your old love letters to me."

"Those were Christmas decorations, for your information. They'd started looking a little stale."

"Oh?" he said, looking faintly amused. "Was there a Christmas tree, too?" When she nodded, he kissed her. "I found the present you bought for me, and I couldn't resist opening it. I'm glad you didn't throw *it* away, too."

"Do you like it?"

"It's wonderful," he said.

"I bought it on impulse. To tell you the truth, I'd forgotten whether you smoked. I tried to remember if you'd smoked on our first date, but it seemed a million years ago. Ronald Colman smokes. But of course you aren't Ronald Colman," she said. "You're much more . . .heartless."

"What are you talking about? I *don't* smoke," my father said.

"Your gift!" she exclaimed. "The sterlng-silver cigarette case. What did you think I was talking about?"

"The sterling-silver picture frame. *This*," he said, digging the case from one trouser pocket. "I'll admit it's an unusual design for a picture frame, sort of a man-size locket without a chain. You can carry it around like a wallet and just flip it open whenever you get lonesome. *Voila*!" He opened the case, and inside, tucked neatly into the rectangular space, was my mother's photograph.

They strolled back to the Quonset hut, arm in arm, and he talked about the plane crash and its aftermath. Not a single life had been lost, and all of the injured would recover. She heard the vibrancy of doctorly pride in his voice. Even the boy he'd almost lost was getting married tomorrow. The fellow's young bride-to-be was flying to Guam for a bedside ceremony. "Now I can relax," he said. "The emergency has passed."

They reached the doorway of the Quonset hut, and my father picked her up and carried her ceremoniously across the threshold. A lumpish-looking piece of fruit swung over her head, and she ducked.

"What's that?" she asked, pointing.

He laughed. "It's a piece of passion fruit," he said with a wink. "In lieu of mistletoe."

Winter Woods

Shelby Stephenson

Out of what white country, snow
reaches rotted apples still on stem in the
    valley.
Wind laughs like a giant breathing from a
    cavern.
Firs hold snowshapes:
white gingerbread men in crabapple trees,
foxes and geese lost from all but their tracks
and glances from leaves penduluming the air.

Journey of the Magi

Michael Chitwood

On the last day of classes before Christmas break, Frank always taught T.S. Eliot's "Journey of the Magi" to his freshmen. "Give them something to chew on besides home cooking," he would say to Carol, his wife. The poem, from the point of view of one of the three "Wise Men," is wonderfully ambiguous, Frank tells his students. He likes its honesty, he says, but what he really likes is its bitterness and carping. "A cold coming we had of it,/Just the worst time of the year/ For a long journey, and such a long journey:/ The ways deep and the weather sharp,/ The very dead of winter." He liked watching that opening fall on them like an icy snow. It was a counter balance to what he imagined their cheery little communities to be. Their whiteGingher frame churches festooned with pine sprays, their "live" nativity scenes and off-key Christmas cantatas. In his mind, he created for each student a version of Carol's rural North Carolina birthplace, the backwater where he would spend the break with her hard-working, clean-living dairy-farmer parents. He was the flip side of the parent coin for "his kids"—tough, willing to think critically. No easy unexamined faith for him.

Frank met Carol when she was in her senior year and he was a graduate teaching assistant. He had been attracted to her from the first day of class, but it was her optimistic reading of the Eliot poem, which he was teaching for the first time, that had absolutely captivated him. He asked her out for coffee after that class and wound up driving her home that year, and every year since.

"Then at dawn we came down to a temperate valley,/ Wet, below the snow line, smelling of vegetation,/ With a running stream and a water-mill beating the darkness/ and three trees on the low sky./ And an old white horse galloped away in the meadow." Frank couldn't now read the second stanza without thinking of the trip to Carol's folks' place.

There was even a deserted mill and always somewhere along the way a sway-backed horse alone in a pasture.

The tight community of farmers and mill hands was a safe, solid place to grow up, Frank knew. And Carol's optimism sprang from the very ground there; it flavored the water, just like the tin dipper that Carol's father still used at the barn. But it was all a little much for Frank, the jolly family dinners, without good wine, the endless talk of weather and which cow had freshened or would soon. He always made sure he brought a stack of academic journals along, to catch up on his reading he would say. But really he needed articles with titles like "The Myth of Text: The Fallacy of Authorship as Subtext to a Multicultural Re-evaluation of the Canon" to counterweight Carol's mother's talk of her prayer circle and her desire for grandchildren. Grandchildren! Frank would never be that optimistic.

The annual journey to Carol's house was, for Frank, time travel. The years, it seemed to him, began to roll back as soon as they left their progressive university town. By the time they had crossed two county lines, passing farm houses, feed stores and log tobacco barns, Frank was sure that they had retreated decades, maybe even centuries. And he could never predict what awaited him in this past.

"Frank, we'll need you tonight. Mr. Webster fell and broke his hip, you know he may have to have one of those steel pins put in it, I tell you when they start wiring me together like a busted baling machine I'm just going to go out behind the barn and put an end to it," Carol's father said in his typically round-about and overly descriptive way. Frank wasn't sure how Mr. Webster's accident related to him.

"Howard Webster has always been our third wise man. Frank will have to fill," Carol's father continued. It wasn't a question. Carol's smirk showed Frank that she wasn't going to intercede; she was enjoying this. She even found one of her father's old bathrobes for Frank to wear. Her father, of course, would wear the newest one.

The church was always packed for the Christmas Eve service. The crush of potato-and-gravy-fat worshippers, in combination with the oil furnace, had the sanctuary in a swelter. At least it seemed so to Frank, already in a sweat beneath the red velour bathrobe. He held an empty El Producto cigar box, which had been covered with Reynolds Wrap. On each side of him were portly men in multi-colored bathrobes, one holding a Styrofoam Christmas ball to which rhinestones had been glued, the other clutching a large perfume bottle containing water tinted with red food coloring.

As the congregation began "We Three Kings," Frank and his fellow Magi trooped down the aisle. They took their places at the side of the manger scene, which featured a twelve-year-old Mary, a fourteen-year-old Joseph, some children on their hands and knees wearing capes to which cotton balls had been affixed. Sheep, Frank thought. And, Oh God, Frank almost said aloud, a real infant.

The preacher droned from Luke. Frank felt faint. ". . .Were we led all that way for birth or death?" He silently rehearsed Eliot's lines. Sweat ran down his back and trickled from his hair onto the thick velour collar. "I had seen birth and death. . .this birth was hard and bitter agony for us, like Death, our death."

The infant whimpered and then set in to a determined crying. Mary looked to the three wise men for help. The sheep giggled. The crying was drowning out the gospel reading. Mary fidgeted. Joseph stepped back from the manger, as if to leave. The preacher got louder, reading now what sounded like nonsense to Frank. The baby's crying seemed patterned, in measured bursts like iambic pentameter. Mary's face contorted and she looked to Frank, her eyes begging.

Frank was suddenly watching himself act. He took a half-step forward, placed his silver gift beside the manger and picked up the child. He rocked the baby in his arms and it quieted. He looked into the red chubby faces of the innocents all around him as they sang, "Oh Holy Night." They hadn't seen the death. They acted as if nothing unusual had happened. But they seemed to know how glad the young king was beneath his royal robe.

Angels

(for my sister)

Rebecca McClanahan

Only an angel fresh from a fall
would know how far we have come
from that summer when the sky
forgot to open, nothing above our heads
but sleek plastic tubes that fed your heart.
And me like Jacob beside you,
my head on a stone pillow.
Ninety times I changed the needle
and slipped it into your veins,
watching you sleep, your skin's pallor.
Night by night I practiced
how to give you up.
I would empty you from my arms
and fill them with your daughter.
When I held her, it was you I saw,
thirty years ago. I was on tiptoe,
watching through the slats of your crib,

waiting your next breath.

The angel of Ezekiel had four faces:
lion, ox, eagle, man
and the feet of a grazing calf.
They say the first angels were wingless
like distant cousins visiting, no trumpets.
Of the nine heavenly choirs,
only the lowliest touch up.
Their name means messenger.
I have seen museum angels
reaching out with all they have left,
stumps and hollow sockets.
The years have worn their faces smooth.
It might be any eyes here—
your daughter, our grandmother
looking down. Those nights
by your bed, smoothing the linen,
I tried to call back faces,
remembering the halo Mother made,
how she twisted a wire circle
while Father bent a coat hanger
into wings that he strapped on my back
for the pageant where I was the smallest
angel singing Midnight Clear.
The straps dug into my back.
That is what I remembered

until you touch me from the bed
and I turned to see the stone rolled away
like Mary, bearing spices for the dead,
who walked past the risen one,
thinking he was the gardener.
Surrounded by seraphim hosts of light,
she walked right past.

Christmas with Dylan

Bland Simpson

"A little more to the left."

"No. It's fuller around to the right."

"You're crazy."

"Just try it my way and you'll see."

"Now the stand's leaking."

"Somebody's liable to get electrocuted."

"I swear you've got the best side to the wall."

"I thought we'd be through by now."

"You're right—it was better back to the left."

"Oh, god. I've already gone and tied it to the wall sconce."

It was a few days before Christmas, 1968, and my family had gathered. The living room was filled with the intense clean resinous smell of the tree. Once we had it hoisted into place, we set about the bristly business of decorating. I was twenty, and my mind was full of music. Withdrawing to the sofa, I thought: *Bob Dylan wouldn't be caught dead doing this.*

"The angel's crooked."
"Let's not have the angel this year."
"Not have the angel?!"

I decided to make a pilgrimage to Woodstock, New York, to see Dylan. It didn't slow me down a bit that I had little to tell the man except that I was inspired by his song writing. To shake Dylan's hand, that would be Christmas enough.

The next afternoon, with no more than fifty dollars, I set out. I was catching a ride north with two friends from UNC, paying my share of all the twenty-six cents per gallon gas we'd burn, and coming back south by thumb. Fifty dollars would be plenty.

This was really my second pilgrimage to Dylan and Woodstock. The first I had undertaken several weeks before, during Thanksgiving, and had abandoned outside of East

Stroudsburg, Pennsylvania. I got cold and lost my nerve on a little-traveled high-ridge country road there, and I turned back. On the way home I caught a ride with a black schoolteacher, who carried me all the way down 81 through the Shenandoah Valley night. We drank a beer together the last hour before he let me out, and agreed that things might be getting better between the races, or at least we *hoped* they were.

Then a trucker hauled me from Hillsville down the Blue Ridge mountains. When we stopped at a Mt. Airy diner and I didn't order anything, he thought I was broke and made me let him buy me a cup of coffee and a chance on a punchboard. Back in the semi, he gave me some liquor, which I drank from a six-ounce hillbilly souvenir jug he'd stashed under the seat. He let me off at 52 and 40 in Winston-Salem about four in the morning.

Immediately a hunter with an enormous buck strapped to the top of his Impala picked me up. A couple minutes later he said: "Look, I hope this don't bother you none but I got to hear some music." He popped an eight-track of Johnny Horton's *Greatest Hits* into the tapeplayer, and the car was full of the songs

I'd learned to sing by: "Battle of New Orleans" and "Sink The Bismarck!" and "North To Alaska." The teacher and the trucker and the Horton-loving hunter made me think better of the pilgrimage business. I forgot the Stroudsburg cold and knew I'd try again.

It was several weeks later, the evening of December 10th, when we piled into my friend's '65 Rambler and went roaring up the three-laned U.S. 1, which is these days a ghost road just south of the Petersburg Turnpike. On and on, all night, the first of many deep and dreamless long-haul trips up and down the Eastern Seaboard. I was astounded at the size and magnificence of the great bridge at Wilmington, aghast at the dazzling lunar landscape, gas flares and chemical air of north Jersey. One of my more worldly companions gazed upon the scene and remarked with a combination of pride and disgust: "America flexing her muscles!"

From the George Washington Bridge we looked out over the vast glare of Manhattan. In less than a year it would be my home, but that night it made me feel thoroughly out of place, for a few moments sorry I had even come. Soon it was past, and we were in the dark Connecticut country, and it was snowing lightly. I recovered my spirits; after all, I was on a mission.

They were driving me towards Storrs, Connecticut, to see the Hickey family, late of Chapel Hill, and coincidentally to perform a flanking maneuver—to approach Woodstock from the north and east. The plan had been to leave me in New Haven where the big roads fork, but at the last minute my compatriots, who were bound for Boston, found it in themselves to veer off to the north and take me right into Storrs.

They left me at a gas station at first light, a gray dawning, six or eight inches of snow on the ground and more still coming down. I showed up oafish and unannounced at the Hickeys' home between eight and nine in the morning, four days before Christmas. They masked whatever annoyance they might have felt and greeted me affectionately.

All four daughters in the Hickey family were home for Christmas except the one who drew me there. She wasn't expected for another twenty-four hours or so. No matter. The other three were going ice-skating that day, and so, now, was I. Most folks don't forget their first time on ice-skates, and with good reason.

Sue did finally come home, and we had a lovely New England time that next day. It was brisk, and the sun was bright on the unmelting snow. She got over the surprise of my presence, commiserated with me about the Tower-of-Babel Christmas tree back home, and wondered what I would say to Bob Dylan, himself, when we met. After breakfast the next morning she drove me out to the highway, and I was soon up at the Massachusetts Turnpike in the company of a Goddard student driving a Volkswagen with skis strapped to the back.

He was on intersession, he told me. He was going somewhere to ski for six or eight weeks, for which he would get academic credit. We drove west towards New York and the Hudson, and, before he left me off at the Saugerties exit, I had seen groves of chalk-white paper birches for the first time.

A couple of artists, a man and a woman, in a dingy old Pontiac drove me from Saugerties to Woodstock. They said they were friends of Bob's, and suddenly everything felt very chummy. The artists called themselves Group Two-One-Two, after the route number of the Saugerties-Woodstock road. A few years later, when I was living on the Upper West Side in New York, I would see a notice in the *Village Voice* about a show they were having down in SoHo and meant to ramble down and take a look. But the notice would stay taped up on the refrigerator until well past the closing of their show, and I would never make the trip.

Group Two-One-Two's explanation of where exactly Bob Dylan lived was so convoluted that I stepped into a shop in downtown Woodstock, a bakery, and asked them. In moments I was tromping on out of town through a wood and up a hill towards something called "The Old Opera House." Dylan's driveway, the bakers said, was right across from it.

It was about eighteen or twenty degrees in the middle of the afternoon, and I wasn't used to such cold. I didn't *feel* dressed for it, but I certainly *looked* like I was. I had on a Marine greatcoat from a surplus store south of Wake Forest, a slouch hat from a surplus store on Granby Street in Norfolk that I'd

Simpson

bought on my way to see *Cool Hand Luke* with my Virginia cousins, and a pair of snakeproof boots from Rawlins, Wyoming, that I'd bought on my way to be a cowboy in eastern Montana. (You, or your beneficiary, said the card in the boot box, got a thousand dollars if you died of snakebite while wearing the boots, providing the snake bit you *through* the boots.) All this was practical and, back home in North Carolina, warm winter wear, though my mother lamented that I looked like something from the Ninemiles—a remote swamp in Onslow County down east. It hardly mattered here. In Woodstock everyone looked like something from the Ninemiles.

Without my even thumbing for it someone offered me a ride, and there I was at The Old Opera House. There turned out to be six or eight driveways next to and across from the place, no names on mailboxes, certainly no sign that said: "This way to Bob Dylan's house." I waited. About twenty minutes went by before a thin man in his thirties came striding up the paved road. He would have walked right past me, but I spoke up: "Excuse me, do you know which one of these driveways goes to Bob Dylan's house?"

"This one." He pointed at the one he was starting down.

"Thanks." I fell in beside him, and we walked fifty yards or so before either of us spoke again.

"Is Bob, uh, expecting you?"

"No."

"Hunh. I don't know if it'll be cool for you to just...go up to his house."

This was discouraging, but what could I do? Go back to the bakery and telephone for an appointment? "I've come from North Carolina," I announced.

"Oh." He gave up, and we kept walking. A few hundred yards into the woods the road forked, and he pointed towards a long low building of dark logs that looked like a lodge. "That's Bob's house." Then he disappeared down the other fork.

In the driveway at Bob's house were a '66 powderblue Mustang and a boxy 1940 something-or-other with the hood up. Two men, one of them small and weedy, the other bulky and bearded, were working on the engine. I stomped up in my snakeproof boots, but neither of them looked up. After a minute or two of staring over their shoulders at the old engine, I finally said, quite familiarly, "Bob around?" The weedy man didn't respond, but the big fellow gave a head-point at the log lodge and said, "Yeah."

Sara Dylan answered the door, gave me a blank look, and closed the door. About two minutes later Bob Dylan himself appeared and stepped out onto the small porched entry. He wore blue jeans, a white shirt buttoned all the way up and a black leather vest, and he was very friendly and relaxed.

"Bland. What kind of a name is that?"

A family name, I said. Then just to make sure he'd heard me right, he asked me to spell it.

"Bland. Well, I sure won't forget that." He talked in person just like he sounded on record in "The Ballad of Frankie Lee And Judas Priest."

"North Carolina, that's a long way."

I agreed, but I wanted to meet him, shake his hand, tell him I admired his work, that I wanted to write songs myself.

"What did you want to do before you got this idea about writing songs?"

"I was going to go to law school."

"Well," he said, more serious than not, "country's gonna need a lot of good lawyers. Maybe you ought to keep thinking 'bout that."

This wasn't what I had traveled hundreds of miles to hear. I started asking questions. Did he live in Woodstock all the time? Most of the time, he said, but he was thinking about moving to New Orleans. When would he have a new record out? In the spring—"I'm real happy with this one." He was talking about "Nashville Skyline," which he had just finished. I asked about a song of his the Byrds had recorded, a song I'd heard out in Wyoming the summer before. "Yeah, I know the one you mean, but I can't call the name of it right now—it's in there somewhere." The song was the riddle-round "You Ain't Going Nowhere."

We talked along like that for almost forty-five minutes, during which time I felt the cold acutely. Dylan was dressed in shirtsleeves, but he didn't seem to notice the cold at all. He must have known my head was full of hero-worship, and he was kind enough to let my time with him be unhurried. The moment of my mission played out as naturally as the tide. I was immensely grateful, am grateful yet.

The pilgrim was ready to go home. I pulled my map out, unfolded it, and while we talked about what the best way to head back south was, the bulky fellow lumbered over from the old car where he and the weedy man had been working all the time. The mechanic ignored me, and I ignored him right back, which was easy enough: I had the entire eastern United States spread out in front of me. My mind was on the road, but I did want one last word or two with Bob Dylan. He gave Dylan a report on all the things that weren't wrong with the car, then said: "I think we can get it started if we hook it up to the battery charger."

"Okay," Dylan said. "It's in the garage."

"I got it already, and tried to hook it up, but even with that long cord it won't reach. We need another extension cord."

"Extension cord," Dylan said, and looked past the big man at the old car. He thought about the request a few moments, then shook his head.

"Gee, Doug," he said, "I'm afraid we just used the last extension cord on the kids' Christmas tree."

Christmas Poem

Stephen Smith

I cannot write a Christmas
poem for you,
not with all those slick verses
oozing through the mail,
the schmaltzy music whining
on the radio.

But what I can do
is tell you of a December
afternoon in 1957
when I sat in Miss Judy's
fourth grade class
listening to the radiators clank
and staring at my scarred desktop
and how Danny Chapman,
hunched in the seat beside me,
looked up suddenly and whispered,

Smith

"It's snowing!"

I looked up too,
along with the rest of the class,
out the tall warped windows,
across the empty playground
to Idlewild Avenue,
and saw that it was true:
the first graywhite dust just drifting
the blue cedars.

If you are an old believer,
even on this bluest of December days,
I would give you that pale afternoon,
the chalkdust scuffle of shoes
on the worn floor,
those children's faces
eager as light.

Rich in Spirit
Ruth Moose

"Lutie." Mrs. Jackson came out of the principal's office and shut the door firmly behind her. "I've got to lock up now." She jangled keys like a charm bracelet. Over her arm hung a white umbrella.

If I had that umbrella, Lutie thought, *I'd be like a mouse under a toadstool, safe and dry. Or I could grab its stem and let the wind blow me home.*

"Whose room are you in this year?" Mrs. Jackson asked, twirling the umbrella.

"Miss Peacock's." Lutie traced the letters on the cover of her book—a battered old copy of Andersen's *Fairy Tales*. *I hate Miss Peacock*, she thought. *I will never, ever forgive her.*

"Has the rain slacked up any?" Mrs. Jackson pushed aside the red paper bells covering a window and peered out. "It's rained cats and dogs all day. Hasn't stopped once." She straightened the bells. "Is someone coming to pick you up?"

"No, ma'am."

"You should have a raincoat. Something on your feet if you must walk."

Lutie shoved her books under the baggy sweater she had on, buttoned her coat that was really meant for spring, and ducked out the door. She heard Mrs. Jackson cluck, "Some mothers don't care."

She does care, Lutie thought, hitting the first puddle with a splat that freckled her legs. *My mother does care. She made me wear her black sweater under my coat to try and keep the wind from blowing through me.* But, oh, how she wished Mama's sweater wasn't black! Susan Reys had a pink sweater. Sometimes Lutie touched it in the coat closet. Soft as the fuzz on a baby's head. Now Lutie pushed her sweater sleeves up and began walking.

"Merry Christmas," Mrs. Jackson called out behind her. Lutie turned and saw the mushroom of the white umbrella bob as Mrs.

Jackson came down the school steps. Then Lutie started to run—past the preacher's house, past the big magnolia tree, past where the barking black dog lived. She stopped at the corner, her heart whirling like Mama's eggbeater when she made it go fast. Lutie took a deep breath of cold air. It didn't matter if she ran. She was going to get wet anyway.

So she walked slowly and stepped on the cracks. "Bruce Williams," she said on the first crack, jinxing him. The next crack was Rachel Jones, then Susan, then Ann, then everybody in her whole class at school, and Miss Peacock, too. She stepped on Miss Peacock twice before starting over. "Bruce Williams." Lutie thought she maybe hated him most of all. He had started it, pointing at her slip hanging out from under her too-small dress. "Look," he'd called, and the whole class had laughed and stared. "Stare, stare, stare," Lutie said, stepping on more cracks.

Lutie looked at the sky, silver gray melting into drops that fell on her head scarf, ran down her face and soaked through her clothes. She clutched her books tighter, jumping over the cracks now. *I'll never stand up at story hour again*, she decided, *and everybody knows the stories I tell are the best.*

Rain ran inside her collar and Lutie lifted her wet hair and tossed her head. She opened her mouth, let in big drops, held them and tasted. Wood smoke. That's how rain tasted, and Lutie bet she was the only person in the world who knew that. She hummed and started to skip, but her feet slid inside her heavy, wet shoes.

At the corner, she turned and walked in the squishy grass beside a gravel street. There was car grease in the puddles, shiny blue rings. She passed by the boarding house and saw that the shades were all down, like eyes closed, sleeping, but electric candles glowed in every window.

In the Barkers' yard, two tricycles lay with their tires pointed at the sky. Lutie's brother Robbie had begged for a tricycle for Christmas, but Mama said no, they couldn't afford it this year.

The Fenders had their door decorated with shiny red paper and a green ribbon. A roof over the wide porch kept it dry and clean. For a moment, Lutie wanted to go stand on that dry, clean porch, too, but she knew she would still be cold. Home would be warm, and it wasn't far now.

Holding her books tight, Lutie ran again, ran and ran against the wind until her face burned and her chest felt squeezed. She tripped on the wet porch step and almost fell.

Mama was at the door in a flash. "Come in quick, honey, and let's get those wet things off you," she said. She shut out the rain and tugged off Lutie's scarf. "You must be soaked to the skin." Mama unbuttoned the light green coat Aunt Helen had sent last winter, back before Daddy had died. It had come in a box with cousin Martha's frilly, outgrown dresses that were "too sweet to be thrown away."

"Mama, you know what?" Lutie wanted to tell her mother how rain tasted.

"Shhh." Her mother slipped off the wet coat. "Robbie and the baby are asleep. Don't wake them." She shook the coat, its arms limp and flapping. "Hope it doesn't shrink. It's almost too small for you now—you won't be able to wear it come spring."

Lutie pulled her books from under her sweater. Their covers were soft, the corners starting to curl. "The books aren't too wet."

"That's the only thing," her mother said. She fitted the coat on the back of a chair and moved it nearer to the wood stove to dry.

Lutie sat in the rocking chair, and her mother pulled off her shoes. "I hope you don't catch pneumonia." She set the shoes on the brick hearth. "We'll dry them a little away from the heat, and maybe they won't be ruined. You'll have to wear them anyway, though. We can't afford another pair just now."

Lutie peeled off her socks. They were cold like the rain, and clung to her skin. Her mother took them and laid them across the stove-pipe.

From the closet, Mama got a ragged pair of dark felt slippers and handed them to Lutie. "Now get that dress off," Mama said, frowning. "Turn around and I'll undo the buttons and sash."

The sash tickled Lutie's legs. She reached for it and wove pink cloth through her fingers as Mama unbuttoned. This was her favorite dress. A floaty one, with flowers and butterflies, that had come in the box with the green coat. It was the dress that had caused all the trouble—but Lutie couldn't tell Mama about it because this morning they'd argued when Lutie had wanted to wear it. "That's a summer dress," Mama had said. "And it's tight on you. Wear something warmer." Then Mama got busy with the baby, and Robbie hurt his foot, so Lutie put on the dress anyway. By the time Mama noticed, it was too late to change, so she made Lutie put on the sweater, the ugly, old black sweater.

"I didn't know this dress was so short," Mama said now. "Did you go around all day with your slip hanging out?"

"No," Lutie mumbled, tasting cloth and starch as she pulled the dress over her head. With her face covered, she felt invisible. Like she wished she had been today. Instead, she had run from the classroom into the girls' bathroom and cried with her head against the wall. "Mama," she said—but her mother had turned away. And anyway, how could she tell her mother she had cried at school? Mama would say she was too big to cry. That what happened wasn't a thing to cry about. That she wasn't a baby anymore.

Her mother took the dress, examined the white line of last year's hem. "I can't let it down anymore, Lutie," she said. "You'll have to stop wearing it. You're growing like a weed." Then she bundled Lutie into her blue chenille robe that smelled of milk. "What are those safety pins doing in your slip, sweetie?"

"Miss Peacock put them there." Lutie undid a pin and handed it to her mother, then another. She remembered Miss Peacock's handkerchief, cool and smelling like lilacs, wiping away the tears.

"That was nice of her, wasn't it?" Mama said.

"Yes," Lutie answered quietly. *Miss Peacock acted so nice*, Lutie thought. *Her hair was so pretty when she bent over, pinning and pinning. But she wasn't nice. Not really.*

Mama put the dress on a hanger and hung if from the mantel. "Looks like somebody could have given you a ride home."

Who? Lutie wanted to ask—*I'm the girl they laughed at. Standing in front of the room saying, "Once upon a time. . ." before Bruce Williams called out, "Look at Lutie's slip!"*

"You had to walk all the way home in that pouring-down rain." Mama shook her head.

"It's okay." Lutie rolled a ball of chenille fuzz. "I didn't mind." She liked being by herself. There was nobody to laugh at her. Nobody to offer fake pity. At first, when they had said they were sorry, Lutie felt warm inside and smiled. But when the bell rang, Bruce elbowed Albert and said, "You didn't tell Lutie."

"Tell Lutie what?"

"Tell her you were sorry. Miss Peacock said everyone had to do it."

Had to tell Lutie! Miss Peacock said! Lutie burned. *I hate them all*, she thought. *Let them beg me to stand up and tell another one of my stories. I won't, never ever again. Let Bruce, let Ann, let Susan, let somebody else try to tell one as good.* Lutie curled her feet under her. "It was fun walking in the rain," she said.

"Fun? Walking in the freezing rain?" Mama hugged her. "Sweetie, sweetie." She brushed Lutie's damp hair back from her forehead. "If you had a real raincoat, it wouldn't be quite so bad."

They had looked at raincoats in the Sears, Roebuck catalog when Mama borrowed a copy from Mrs. Barker. There was a blue one, warm-looking, with a hood, in sizes six to twelve. Lutie asked Mama what size she would take. "About an eight," Mama said and closed the book. They didn't have the money to order one.

"Maybe somebody will send you a raincoat for Christmas," Mama said now.

Lutie knew her mother meant Aunt Helen, Daddy's rich sister in Maine. Closing her eyes, Lutie tried hard to remember her daddy. He was tall, his hair was dark, and he had thin lips that didn't smile much. Sometimes Lutie thought he wasn't dead at all, just gone to Texas, like he did one time before. He said that's where jobs were. But there hadn't been any jobs after all. Just more trying to scrape by once he got home—and then the accident in the spring.

Lutie opened her eyes and studied the flowers on Mama's dress. They used to be purple. Now they were gray and the leaves were worn away. Gone. Like in winter—only real leaves came back, and flowers, too. Mama's flowers just got more and more gray, like cold rain.

Her mother turned away, reached into the crib and covered the baby. Robbie was a lump under the quilt on the big bed. "We'll have an early supper." Mama looked out the window. "Get something hot in you, and maybe you won't catch cold." They would have vegetable soup, Lutie knew, with fat lockets of lima beans and floating okra wheels.

While Mama cooked, Lutie rolled up her

hair on strips of brown paper. Tomorrow she would have curls. Not stiff pigtails. She wouldn't mind the pigtails if she could wear bows on them. Susan Reys had bows. A different bow every day to match her dresses. Lutie decided if there was a bow on her Christmas present, she would wear it in her hair.

On Christmas Eve morning, the mailman brought a box from Aunt Helen, marked DO NOT OPEN UNTIL DECEMBER 25TH. He set it on the floor, under the table where they had a little spike of a cedar tree. Lutie and Robbie had made paper chains and cut out stars and snowflakes for decorations.

"Bike," Robbie crowed, and sat down on the box.

"No," Mama said, laughing. "It's not big enough for a bike."

Lutie tried to lift the box. "It's heavy. What do you think it is?"

"Clothes, I hope," Mama said. "That's what we need. All of us. Some things to keep us warm."

"Are clothes that heavy?" Lutie asked.

"If they're sturdy ones."

Robbie made motor noises and Mama said he had to get off the box.

"Maybe there's a raincoat in there," Lutie said. In her imagination, she saw a blue one, like the one in the Sears catalog, folded into a neat square. There would be a sweater for Mama, too. Yellow or pink. And a pretty new dress.

"I hope there's shirts for Robbie," Mama said, jerking his T-shirt down over his belly. But it rode back up and Lutie could see his puckered navel. So she pictured a nice red shirt for him—red was his favorite color.

On Christmas morning, Lutie slipped from under her quilt and touched her toes to the cold floor. Under the tree, she saw the toy truck she had found for Robbie's gift. She had spotted it, thrown away, half-buried along the roadside. She and Mama washed and scrubbed it with a brush till it was as good as new. Next to the truck was Lutie's old doll, Amy. She had a beautiful new dress made from the blue blouse Lutie had worn in first grade. Mama must have sewn it while Lutie was at school. Lutie picked up Amy, fluffed the dress, then opened the box of peppermint sticks. There were ten each for her and Robbie—and marshmallows for the baby.

After Robbie got his truck and raced it across the floor, and after mama changed the baby, everyone gathered around the box from Aunt Helen. Mama cut the string with a knife. Then Lutie tore off the brown paper and pulled out the smaller boxes inside—one for each of them.

Lutie's gift was wrapped in shiny red paper, with a pretty green ribbon she would save for her hair. She slid the wrapping off carefully, trying not to tear it, and saw the words *Little Women*. "Mama," she said, "I got a book! A brand new book."

Robbie's present was a book, too. About animals. "See the horse, Robbie?" Lutie asked, turning pages. "See the cows and pigs?"

The baby's book was cloth. There was a picture of a shoe, and a real shoelace to tie and untie. "He can learn from it, Mama," Lutie said. The baby chewed the cover, patted the pages and laughed.

Mama sat silent, hands folded loosely on her own package.

"Open yours. Let's see what you got," Lutie

said. When Mama didn't move, Lutie slipped the ribbon off for her, carefully split the tape, and pulled out a red and white book. "A cookbook," Lutie said. She flipped a few pages. "These apples look so real. Robbie, come see what Mama got." She turned more pages. "Look, Robbie."

"Of all the things we need," Mama said in a low voice, "of all the things."

That's what Mama had said when Aunt Helen sent Mama's birthday present last February: a big gold box of chocolate candies shaped like boats and seashells and roses. And Daddy had said how Aunt Helen just didn't know how it was. . . .

"Of all the things," Mama said again. "How could she think, with your daddy gone. . . ." Her voice trailed off.

Lutie looked in the bottom of the big brown box and saw that Aunt Helen had put some balloons in there, and whistles made of paper that rolled out and back like sassy tongues when you blew them. Lutie and Robbie blew and blew the whistles until Mama put her hands over her ears and said, "Enough. Enough, now."

"Look," Lutie said, opening the cookbook

for Mama to see. "Roast beef."

Robbie came over and turned a page. "Chocolate cake, " he said.

"Yum, yum," Lutie said, trying to make Mama smile.

The baby crawled up and grabbed Mama's knee. "Ummmm." He put a finger in his mouth.

Robbie and Lutie laughed. "Look, candy and cookies and. . .yum, yum."

Suddenly Lutie saw dark circles, like lead pennies, hit the page. "Mama," Lutie said. Her mother *never* cried. Not even when the man came to tell them about Daddy. She'd made a deep sound in her throat, and then Robbie had cried and Lutie, and the baby. But not Mama. And Mama didn't cry, either, the time she cut her hand cooking and the blood ran and ran. "Mama!" Lutie said again, scared.

Then Mama stood quickly and smoothed her skirt. "My goodness," she said, picking up the baby. "Look at you, crawling around in your pajamas, barefooted on this cold floor. And me, I haven't got the oatmeal on to cook." She jiggled the baby and he gave a happy shriek. "We'll have raisins in our oatmeal this morning," Mama said, trying out a small smile. "And brown sugar, too. After all, it's Christ-

107

mas."

"And coffee, Mama," Lutie said. "Can I have coffee?"

"Yes." Her mother whirled the baby. "We'll all have coffee."

"Me too." Robbie grabbed her leg. She ruffled his hair as she set the baby down, then put her arms around Lutie. "My big girl."

Lutie leaned against her. "I know why Aunt Helen sent you a cookbook." She felt her mother stiffen. "Because you're such a good cook."

"Oh." Her mother gave a tight little laugh. "You think so?"

"Yes," Lutie said. "You make the best divinity." Mama said divinity was mostly egg whites and lots of beating. Last week, Lutie had helped. Beating, beating until her arms felt heavy enough to drop. But the little puffs of divinity were like magic clouds. They put them into a coffee can, wrapped it with brown paper, and mailed it to Aunt Helen. "It's not much," Mama said. "But we give as best we can."

"Aunt Helen meant well," Lutie said now.

Mama just looked at her for a minute. Then she said, "It was nice of Aunt Helen to remember us, wasn't it?"

"They must be very, very rich," Lutie said. She recalled the pictures Aunt Helen had sent; the big two-story house with the wide front yard.

"Yes, I guess so." Mama pushed Lutie's hair off her face. "But she doesn't have you."

"Or Robbie, or the baby or. . . ."

"Oatmeal for breakfast." Mama bent down and hugged Lutie and Robbie and the baby, too. "A big, healthy hug," she said. "That's what I need. That's the best present." The baby started to squirm and then Robbie reached for his truck. Mama kissed the top of Lutie's head and went to make breakfast.

Lutie rubbed the smooth cover of her own book. *I can put my name in this book*, she thought. *I won't have to turn it in to the library. I can keep it forever.* She opened to the first page and began to read: "'Christmas won't be Christmas without any presents,' grumbled Jo, lying on the rug. 'It's so dreadful to be poor!' sighed Meg, looking down at her old dress. . . ."

Lutie kept reading, and as she read, she felt the words warming and feeding her spirit. *This is going to be a good book*, Lutie thought. *All of it. Every last page.*

The Tree and Its Light

Julian Mason

We placed the Christmas tree for our
Convenience, where it would not be
In the way as we passed, pursuing
The season. That was the only reason
For its site in the front hall corner.
But when we turned-on its lights we
Were amazed at how they seemed to be
Seen from every angle, partly because
Of the convergence of passageways,
But also because of being mirrored
By a picture glass in one direction,
By a mirror in the other, and by
The front window and storm door too.
And when the curtains were opened at
Night the colored light reached out
Beyond the house to the yard, and even
To the cars passing in the street.

Mason

This was no passive light, but light
Seeking, particularly across the
Shadow of night, for something, for
Anything that might accept and send on
Its greeting of expectation of goodness
Resurrected, from one green Christmas
Tree and its small lights reflected.

Santa's Coming, Regardless

Robert Inman

It starts every year, without fail, the day after Thanksgiving. Grownups begin to threaten young people over Santa Claus. The air is full of dire predictions about what might happen Christmas Eve if children aren't something close to saintly. It is the bludgeon used to produce clean plates at mealtime, tidy rooms, impeccable manners and timely homework.

Of course, adults have been putting the evil eye on children's behavior since time immemorial. My grandmother, for example, had a special word of terror for young folks who trampled her flowers, tracked mud on her rug, or swung too high in her porch swing. "Nasty stinkin' young'uns," she'd bark, "I'm gonna pinch your heads off." Mama Cooper was a sweet and kind person who never would have pinched the head off a radish, much less a child, but she could strike fear into her grand-children. We were careful around her flow-ers, her rug and her porch swing.

So the grownup weapon of fear is a time-honored tradition. But the direst predictions of ruin and misfortune, it seems, are always saved for the Christmas season. "If you don't clean up your plate, Santa Claus won't come." "Act ugly one more time, buster, and you'll find a bag of switches under the tree for you on Christmas morning." Well, baloney.

I came to my senses about the Santa Claus business when I met Jake Tibbetts, a crotchety old newspaper editor who appeared in my imagination one day and then took over the pages of my first novel, *Home Fires Burn-ing*. Jake had a built-in bull-hockey detector, and he could spot nonsense a mile away. Jake's grandson Lonnie lived with Jake and his wife Pastine, and when Christmas rolled around, Mama Pastine put the pox on Lonnie about Santa's upcoming visit.

At the breakfast table one morning, Lonnie let a mild oath slip from his ten-year-old lips. Mama Pastine pounced. "Santa Claus has no truck with blasphemers," she said.

"Hogwash," Daddy Jake snorted. "Santa Claus makes no moral judgments. His sole responsibility is to make young folks happy. Even bad ones. Even TERRIBLE ones."

"Then why," Lonnie asked, "does he bring switches to some kids?"

Jake replied, "This business about switches is pure folklore. Did you ever know anybody who really got switches for Christmas? Even one?"

Lonnie couldn't think of a single one.

"Right," said Daddy Jake. "I have been on this earth for sixty-four years, and I have encountered some of the meanest, vilest, smelliest, most undeserving creatures the Good Lord ever allowed to creep and crawl. And not one of them ever got switches for Christmas. Lots of 'em were *told* they'd get switches. Lots of 'em laid in their beds trembling through Christmas Eve, just knowing they'd find a stocking full of hickory branches come morning. But you know what they found? Goodies. Even the worst of 'em got some kind of goodies. And for one small instant, every child who lives and breathes is happy and good, even if he is as mean as a snake every other

115

instant. That's what Santa Claus is for, any-how."

Well, Daddy Jake said it better than I ever could. I believe with all my heart that he is right, just as I have always believed fervently in Santa Claus and still do.

I believed in Santa Claus even through the Great Fort Bragg Misbehavior of 1953. My father was stationed at Fort Bragg with the Army, and I was in the fourth grade at the post elementary school. The day before school let out for the Christmas holidays, Santa Claus landed on the playground in an Army helicopter. It was, to me and my class-mates, something akin to the Second Com-ing. When we went out to welcome Santa, the teachers stationed the first through fourth graders on one side of the playground and the fifth and sixth graders on the other. When Santa's chopper landed, I learned why. We little kids were yelling our heads off for Santa to leave us some goodies under the tree a few nights hence. Across the way, the fifth and sixth graders were yelling, "Fake! Fake!" Some of my classmates were crestfallen. It never fazed me. I figured those big kids were wrong then, and still do. Santa Claus is for real. Just look in a kid's eyes and you'll see him.

(By the way, I'm sure the fifth and sixth graders didn't get switches for Christmas. Maybe they should have, but they didn't.)

Grownups are wrong, too, when they threaten kids with the loss of Santa. Daddy Jake was right. We adult types need to grant the kids their unfettered moment of magic. If they act up, threaten to pinch their heads off. But leave Santa out of it.

Advent

Joseph Bathanti

Shock of wing on water.
Three ring-necks break and spin
into greying and oleander south
and west of us. The blind dog,
haunch high in star-thistle
and what's left of the pearl millet,
has come with me to knock down
the Christmas tree. It was
Advent last he took up with us
and still he lies awake
when other dogs sleep, his eyes
burning like green meteors.

As we navigate the steep pond bank,
he stumbles in horse prints
where they've sunk to the fetlock.
His gait is querulous. Like Isaac,

he intuits the blade is for him.
"Trust," I whisper as I hold
the hatchet over the pink-hearted
cedar and strike.

The heron, having tarried an extra
season in his hideout, lifts up
like an ungainly bomber, marshalling
wings and wading legs before jetting
above the mistletoe, surrendering
to us our season of belief. Over
the river when the tree falls, he
is the bluest thing in Anson today.

The dog lies next to the tree
and noses the perfumed marrow. Smoke
chuffs out of the red house where
the woman sleeps, one hundred years
since a child was born to Grassy Island.
A hawk bellies over fallow fields.
Pilgrims enter Bethlehem.
Beneath my knee, such country exists.

Ellen Foster's Christmas

Kaye Gibbons

Christmas came to my house with the people drinking eggnog and decking the halls on the televison set. I am glad I did not believe in Santa Claus. As my daddy liked to say—wish in one hand and spit in the other and see which one gets full first.

Although I did not believe in Santa Claus I figured I had a little something coming to me. So on Christmas Eve I went with Starletta to the colored store and bought myself some things I had been dying for and paper to wrap them with.

I knew my mama's mama was having her usual big turkey dinner that night but that was OK because I had turkey sliced up with dressing along with two vegetables and a dab of dessert.

As long as there is a parade on the television.

I got Starletta and her mama and daddy a nice spoon rest. When they were not looking I had the sales lady wrap up the one I saw with the green chicken on it. Then I had the rest of the money for my own self.

It made my heart beat fast to shop. The store was all lit up with Christmas cheer and shoppers with armloads of presents.

I got two variety packs of construction paper, a plastic microscope complete with slides, a diary with a lock and key, an alarm clock, and some shoes.

When I got home I wrapped the presents and wondered if I ought to wrap something laying around the house for my daddy. I did not have enough paper. He did not come home that night anyway.

I wrapped them at the kitchen table and hid them.

When I found them the next day I was very surprised in the spirit of Christmas.

Twenty-Six Views of Christmas

Lenard D. Moore

I.
letting her hand go
a cramp in my right side
Christmas chill
as I raise my head
listening to the hush

II.
brief glint
of a glass ornament
beyond reach
yet my leg
keeps stroking hers

III.
deserted street
the yowl of a cat

beneath the Christmas tree
through the cracked window
the children dancing

IV.
empty room
on top of kitchen counter
bowl of tangerines
quickening footsteps coming down
the second story stairs

V.
cutting the fruit cake
my wife whistles to herself
the kettle's silence
on the potbelly stove
in the light of the sun

VI.
one hour later
the answering machine speaks
a Christmas message
the distance in our friend's voice
that crackles, crackles

VII.
a passerby coughs

as twigs snap across the way
Christmas solar light
the raccoon's head shifts
in the hollow tree

VIII.
how the wind
reshapes the Christmas trees
the locks of her hair
first falling of snow
in twilight

IX.
on the table
only a potted poinsettia
struck by dusk light
the small spot darkening
between our feet

X.
in the darkening room
the fireplace glows and glows
stocking on the mantle
she stretches out
on the shiny hardwood floor

XI.
our bowed heads
before the Christmas meal
gleaming glass candles
on the mahogany table
crystal glasses sparkle

XII.
tinsel everywhere
hand-in-hand with her
singing "Merry Christmas"
a picture of us slantwise
on the wall panel

XIII.
spruce after spruce
topped with a glowing angel
couple leaving home
beyond them the moon
and sound of the wind

XIV.
street with noel lights
shining pole to pole
cat's green eyes
through the bare branches
of the maple tree

XV.
yard lamp strung with lights
"Jingle Bells" blasting through
    speakers
of the cold car
slow smoke all day
from the brick red chimney

XVI.
beneath the window
a pile of pine straw
on the old black boot
brightened by the Christmas lights
hooked to the eaves of the house

XVII.
snow on the steps
a Christmas wreath on the door
their laughter greatens
my shadow stretches for the
    doorbell
that glows before the touch

XVIII.
bedtime nears
picking up candy cane wrappers
our eyes meet

with a handful of moonlight
now we close the blinds

XIX.
at the last minute
unplugging the Christmas lights
dropping the plug
I trip over empty boxes
and tiptoe upstairs

XX.
the new negligee
fitting my wife just right
Christmas lunar light
in a corner of the bedroom
a shadow slightly stirs

XXI.
in moonlight
the dark outline of her lips
this Christmas
the cluster of bells
clearly chiming

XXII.
in the brass bed
she slips her hand down my

    stomach
the smell of eggnog
still strong on her breath
as she slowly shifts

XXIII.
late Christmas moon
glowing into the bedroom
again and again
our feet touch
beneath the patchwork quilt

XXIV.
shadow still stirring
on the top of the desk
a Christmas card falls
how heavy the odor
of our lovemaking

XXV.
afterwards
Christmas music still ringing
in my ears
the night's silence deepens
as she sleeps

XXVI.
middle of the night
unwrapping the last gift
my daughter jumps
a glinting gold watch
ticks on

Christmas Letters

Lee Smith

Like me, you probably receive a number of Christmas letters every year. You know the ones I mean—those long, chatty epistles mass-produced on Merry Christmas stationery, full of mostly good news. These letters used to come mimeographed—remember that fading purple ink? Then they were photocopied. . .now they are often typeset on the computer.

Maybe you just shake your head and toss your Christmas letters into the trash. Maybe you really hate them; one of my friends refers to them as the "brag and gag" letters.

Me, I have this compulsion to read them all, every word, several times, even if they are from some distant cousin I scarcely remember, or some couple I met briefly on a trip in 1985 and have never laid eyes on since.

For every Christmas letter is the story of a life, and what story can be more interesting than the story of our lives? Often, it is the life of an entire family. We get the big news—who died, who got married, who had a baby or moved to Texas, all conveyed in that strangely perky tone peculiar to Christmas letters.

But there is always some news that we don't read here, some equally big news which we are not being told, and this is perhaps the most fascinating thing about Christmas letters. Sometimes what is not said is even more important than what is on the page. I read every word and save every one, mulling them over and over.

Since I write Christmas letters myself, I know what's going on here. Denial is at work —that catch-all term for not-knowing or not-admitting. Psychologists are always trying to get us to give up denial; but I think it is often a good and useful thing, keeping us going, allowing us to do what has to be done in the world. Families run on denial—they have to. Actually, the term I prefer is what Ibsen called "the saving lie." These "saving lies" are often the very stuff of Christmas letters.

They're not even lies, not really. When you sit down to write a Christmas letter, you are constructing a story of your life, and it is a true story, though you could write another, different story which would be equally true. And another. And another. And these stories would enrich and inform—rather than disprove—one another. For we are all so various, and our stories are so complex.

Anyway, Christmas letters are written as much for the writer, I believe, as for the recipient. Because Christmas can be dangerous, a scary season, full of loaded traditions and ideas. Writing a Christmas letter forces us to take stock: How do we really feel about our family? Who do we really want to keep in touch with? What part of the past do we want to forget? What part of the past do we want to claim? What is really important to us, anyway? How do we feel about kids, faith, marriage, home? What does success mean? These are the traditional themes of the Christmas letter, and your correspondent is walking through an emotional minefield to get to you. It's hard. We've only got one page to get it right. Or at least to get it as right as we can, which is all anybody can ever do anyway, isn't it? The best we can. For me, the underlying message of any Christmas letter is one of hope—written across the years, across the map. We're still here, and we hope you are. Merry Christmas.

Lullay

Kathryn Stripling Byer

Gone
to straw,
as we say
in these mountains
where cattle
are thought to be
kneeling at this very
moment in tribute
to what she
bore, I let
the tidings of this
holy night wash
me through and
through. Emptied
of all save a voice
winding round me
like swaddling

of scarcely more
subsance than
breath, I will know
how she lay
like a husk swept aside
on the threshing
floor, hearing
somewhere in the darkness
a child whimper. . .

Seasonal Rites

Ellyn Bache

"It's hard to plan a Chanuka party with a Christmas tree going up," Claire teases her husband. "Maybe impossible."

"Then come decorate," says Paul.

"Soon." She's still debating how many pounds of potatoes she'll need for the *latkes*. Temple Shalom's preschoolers won't eat much, but the older ones will inhale all she can make.

Watching Paul attach strings of lights to the tree, Claire feels distracted, expectant, still torn between holidays after fourteen years. People are coming for *hors d'oeuvres* tomorrow, so the decorating must be done. Muriel, the ten-year-old, tenderly unpacks each ornament as Paul works. But Louie, the five-year-old, is unexpectedly napping.

Normally wild with energy, today Louie barely made it through their trip to the Christmas tree farm before falling into this dead sleep. Claire attributes his odd behavior to the antibiotic for his latest strep throat.

"Daddy's almost finished," she says, nudging him. "We can hang the decorations." Paul, who hasn't set foot in church since high school, nevertheless has definite ideas about the tree. It must be white pine; the lights must be placed so they'll illuminate the ornaments from behind—ornaments, Claire fears, as tacky as the ones her mother-in-law always had. Even today, Teresa decorates with every styrofoam snowman and angel her six children ever made. Once, Claire had cringed. But that was before Muriel and Louie arrived, and before she learned to love Teresa.

Still groggy, Louie picks up a crinkled mass of green paper. "My wreath," he grins. Then he drops it to scratch his stomach. "I itch." He lifts his shirt to show the round red welts adorning his ample belly.

"He's getting a rash," Paul says.

"Oh, yuk," says Muriel.

"The antibiotic," Claire tells them. "I'll bet he's allergic. Don't worry, Louie, I'll give you some Benadryl."

Later, she calls Dr. Roberts, who says Claire has done the right thing. Tomorrow Louie should be better. This doesn't temper her alarm at the angry red splotches still popping up on her son's neck and arms.

The next morning he is covered with them. Stomach, legs, even his earlobes. Dr. Roberts says continue the Benadryl and give him a lukewarm bath for the itching.

"Take Muriel to Sunday School," Paul says. "Get out for a while. Come on, Louie, your old Dad's going to give you a bath."

Louie manages a slight, wan smile.

At Temple Shalom, cutouts of Maccabee warriors adorn the walls, and Chanuka items are on sale in the social hall. Claire buys Louie a dreidle, the four-sided top with Hebrew letters on each side, so he can play the traditional game Paul terms "Jewish craps." Though Louie prefers climbing trees to spinning tops, the dreidle should amuse him while he's sick.

Chanuka is weeks away, but Claire checks the temple's kitchen for party equipment: bowls for mixing potatoes with flour and onions, cast-iron skillets for frying the *latkes* in oil. Her own mother never heated the oil enough, so her *latkes* were always greasy. But Claire enjoyed them anyway until the year her father died and her mother stopped celebrating holidays altogether. Claire didn't go to services again until she had children of her own—this year Teresa offered to take Muriel to the Catholic Church. Claire was surprised to hear herself say no. Her parents had raised her Jewish, however haphazardly. She wanted to do the same for her daughter.

"The water helped the rash for a while," Paul says when Claire returns. "But now it's coming back." As the day passes, Louie's welts deepen and spread, and he begins to run a fever.

"How'd you like grandma to sit with you while Mom and I have our party?" Paul suggests finally.

"Sure," Louie says without expression.

On the phone, Teresa says she'll be right over. Having raised her own large family, she relishes still feeling needed.

"Do you want to hear a story?" Claire asks Louie after she's set out the *hors d'ouevres* and dressed. "I can tell about the Maccabees."

"We had that in Sunday school."

"Then you tell _me_ ." But Louie shakes his head.

So Claire begins. In olden times the Syrians wouldn't let the Jewish people pray in their Temple. Finally Judah Maccabee defeated the Syrian army so the Jews could worship again. But when they rekindled the light in their Temple that's never supposed to go out, there was only enough oil for one day.

"And you know what?"

"I know, but you tell it," Louie says listlessly.

"It took eight days to get more oil. But when the oil was brought, the flame in the Temple was still burning."

Louie sighs.

"That's why it's called the miracle of lights. That's why we have eight candles in the menorah and fry _latkes_ in oil."

"And get presents."

"One present, on the first night."

"Michael gets presents all eight nights."

"That's because his parents are both Jewish. He doesn't get to have Santa Claus."

"Oh. Right."

Sometimes Claire fears that, caught between religions, Louie and Muriel will be hope- lessly confused. But so far they glide easily between Passover and Easter, Chanuka and Christmas, drawing sweetness from both. Looking down, Claire sees that Louie has fallen suddenly and peacefully asleep. Maybe it is only the parents who are confused.

"Handling allergies is a science these days," Teresa says after the party. "They'll fix him right up." This because Louie's fever has shot up and now stands at a hundred and three.

"I hope you're right, Teresa." Claire has always addressed her mother-in-law by her first name, even though Teresa once suggested Claire call her *mother*. Tonight, Claire wishes she had.

Dr. Roberts has asked them to bring Louie to his office. Claire and Paul wrap him in a blanket and carry him outside. They don't even put on his shoes.

"These reactions are scary, but usually they're self-limiting," Dr. Roberts says after he gives Louie an adrenaline shot and hands Claire some medicine samples.

"*Breathing* medicine?"

"Just in case fluid builds up in his lungs. You probably won't need it."

Briefly, Claire is visited by the litany of soothing platitudes offered when her mother was sick. "Short-term illness. . .nothing serious." She reminds herself they've been seeing Dr. Roberts for years and have no reason to distrust him.

The next morning Louie's welts are gone, but he's splotchy and a little feverish. Claire tells herself he'll recover in no time. Children do. She wants everything back to normal.

But she is uneasy. Dialing Teresa just to hear her voice, she gets only the answering machine. Teresa must have gone to church. A childish notion strikes her—that if Teresa prays for Louie at St. Ann's and Claire prays at Temple Shalom, they will have a double line, as it were, to God; perhaps He will hear one of them. A silly idea—but she feels much better.

That evening, Louie dozes on Claire's bed as she phones her *latke* party committee. Still asleep, he begins to cough. Not an ordinary cough, but a deep rasp. *Huh, huh, huh.* . .a rolling and rumbling of phlegm, over and over without resolution. As if he's choking on his own lungs.

"Honey, sit up," she says, but he sleeps on, coughing convulsively. "Paul!" she screams.

Paul rushes in, lifts him up. "Wake up, son. Wake *up*." Finally—disoriented, irritable—Louie does.

They give him his medicine, rush him to the car. In the emergency room minutes later, his breathing is less labored, but he's admitted to the hospital anyway.

The next twenty-four hours are a nightmare. Wired into IV tubes and monitors, Louie is examined, poked, pried. At first he cries and vents his anger, but then, seeing that Claire and Paul aren't going to stop the torture, he divorces himself from it all and submits to his treatment as if he were somehow. . .absent.

This strange mood persists even after he's released, after days pass and his fever subsides. He naps, ignores his toys, stares into space.

"Probably a little depression," Dr. Roberts says. "Not unusual. Let him resume a few of his activities."

Claire invents an errand. "Come on Louie,

I'll drop the potatoes at the temple and we'll go to McDonald's."

"I'm not hungry."

"Oh, you'll be surprised." She dresses him for the first time all week. In the temple's kitchen, he slumps onto the floor. "My shoes are too tight," he says.

"But they're new shoes."

"They hurt." She pulls one off. Sure enough, ugly red lines mark where the tongue has pressed in; his whole foot is puffy.

"With a reaction like this, it takes time for the swelling to go down," the doctor insists. But the tests he orders sound ominous, and his warning is bleak. "If anyone ever gave him this antibiotic again, it could be life-threatening."

Claire thinks of her mother's illness, and her stomach contracts like a muscle.

On Friday, Claire goes to services. Muriel's class is helping, reading some of the Hebrew. Claire follows along in English and finds the words soothing, familiar.

You shall love the Lord your God with all your mind, with all your strength, with all your being. She heard this as a child, sitting between her parents, breathing her mother's perfume.

Set these words, which I command you this day, upon your heart. Teach them faithfully to your children; speak of them in your home and on your way. The passage is very beautiful to her; a chant, a hosanna.

Bind them as a sign upon your hand; let them be a symbol before your eyes. But wait—She has done none of this. The thought of her laxness begins to draw off the beauty of the words. Perhaps this is her failing: to have married Paul, to have dangled her children between two religions, to have offered no clarity of thought.

Inscribe them on the doorposts of your house, and on your gates. Take the clear path. Perhaps Louie's illness is her punishment for not doing that.

But this sounds crazy—like some pagan superstition.

During the rabbi's sermon, Muriel begins to fidget. Claire gives her a warning look, then smiles as she remembers Teresa's confession last time they were out for their weekly lunch.

"My six weren't very quiet in church, either," she'd said, whispering conspiratorially as she sipped her wine. "You can't scold them, but you can pinch. It's silent—and nobody sees it."

Claire laughed. She couldn't imagine Teresa pinching! But Teresa nodded emphatically. "Oh yes, I pinched them many times!" They giggled together like schoolgirls.

Now Claire wonders how her closeness to this woman could be wrong. Or her love for Paul, who is religious but not observant. Or her passing down his joyful ritual of the Christmas tree, along with Hebrew lessons and *latkes* and her own ancient faith.

But what if she is wrong?

After the service, everyone asks about Louie. "Wonderful!" they exclaim when they hear he's out of the hospital. But is it? Two weeks ago Louie rode his tricycle down the middle of the street and laughed when she scolded about cars, believing he was invincible. Now this same child is frightened, sick. Louie no longer smiles. Louie cannot fit into his shoes.

A week later, on the first night of Chanuka, they light the menorah and eat roasted chicken Louie picks at and golden *latkes* he doesn't touch. Afterward Louie admires the cars he wanted, but when Muriel suggests they play dreidle, he hasn't the energy.

"I bet you don't even remember what the Hebrew letters stand for on the dreidle," Claire teases.

"They stand for, 'A Great Miracle Happened There,'" he replies, deadpan.

Late that night, Louie wakes her with his coughing. He hasn't slept through a single night without a coughing spell. After giving him his medicine, Claire restlessly stalks the house, touches the cold menorah, picks up the unused dreidle. A Great Miracle Happened There, she thinks. But not here.

On Thursday, Teresa appears at noon, carrying a Greek salad and a bottle of white wine.

"We can't go out, but we still have to eat," she says. While Claire sets out plates, Louie nibbles a peanut butter sandwich as if it were cardboard. The two women exchange glances.

Between them on the table sits Claire's menorah. Though Teresa would never complain, Claire senses that the sight of it hurts her—not so much Claire's Jewishness or Paul's fallen-away Catholicism as the rituals they can't share at a time like this, when they are both so worried.

A sudden memory assails her: of asking her new mother-in-law, fourteen years ago, how she should address her, and of Teresa answering, "Well, *mother* would be nice." But Claire, whose own mother was dying, couldn't do it. Now, for the second time since Louie broke out, she wishes she had. When it comes to religion, Teresa and Claire will always follow different paths. But she might have called Teresa *mother*, they might have shared that. Now salads glisten on their plates, their cups of wine sparkle, and Louie sits pale and ill before them—this child they both love—and it seems fourteen years too late.

The next day, Dr. Roberts discovers Louie's throat culture is still positive for strep. "I think this is what we've been missing. The infection is still there and is feeding into the allergy. In effect, he's allergic to the strep."

To Claire, this sounds ridiculous. So it was

when her mother was sick: one treatment and then another, the diagnosis never really clear.

"What about his shoes?" Dr. Roberts asks as he prescribes another antibiotic. "Do they fit better?"

"I don't know." For days, Claire'd been dressing Louie in Muriel's outgrown slippers. "What if he keeps going down like this?" she asks.

"He's not going down. He's better than he was."

Not much, Claire thinks. Not really.

Louie takes the new medicine, but he doesn't perk up. Mostly he sits in front of the TV, ignoring reruns of Christmas specials he usually adores. Then, late in the week, he sleeps all night without coughing.

"Ten hours straight," Claire reports cautiously when Teresa calls. "But that may not mean anything."

"Well, I prayed for him at Mass." Since the illness, Teresa has gone every morning.

"I should call you Mother Teresa after all this," Claire laughs. "You deserve the Nobel Prize!"

Teresa chuckles. "I always thought it would

be nice to be a nun. Instead I had six kids, and I can't really say I'm sorry."

"Well, maybe not Mother Teresa then. Maybe just *mother*." After so much turmoil, the words have flowed as smoothly as Thursday's wine.

There is a slight pause on the other end. Then Teresa says, a little breathlessly, "Well, that I *would* like."

Louie naps less, sleeps more at night, even stops coughing. But he refuses to dress, and he's so serious Claire can hardly believe he's the same child who a month ago hung from a limb of their oak tree, delighting in her horror.

On the last night of Chanuka, the night of the *latke* party, Claire cleans the food processor she'll take to Temple Shalom to grate the potatoes. In the den, Louie and Muriel watch TV.

"I'm leaving in exactly twenty minutes," she calls to them. "Louie, if you want to go, get ready. I can't be late." She knows she sounds harsh. She also knows Louie will opt to stay home with Paul. The cheerful, buoyant child she knew is gone.

She rinses the processor and listens to snatches of *The Little Drummer Boy* from the other room. She used to like *The Little Drummer Boy* very much—or any stories of miracles, now that she thinks of it. She always hoped some of them were true; she never cared which ones. The Jewish Maccabees, the Christian Nativity. *The Lord is One*, the prayer book said. Back then, she'd believed that any miracle would be proof.

She can see the television dimly from the kitchen: the drummer boy playing for the baby Jesus, offering his meager gift. And now—oh yes, she remembers it very well—right now the drummer boy's little lamb is being healed; this always made her cry. The boy is holding his pet; his gift of love and music has been accepted; the lamb is suddenly well.

"Oh Mommy, do you see *that*?" Louie calls from the den. Even in the flickering light, Claire sees color in Louie's face, notices his smile. And something else: he is fully dressed for the *latke* party. In pants and shirt. And shoes.

"Mommy?" he calls.

But Claire doesn't answer right away because she's standing at the sink with tears running down her cheeks, thinking: I must tell mother, I must tell Paul. In the midst of the confusion there is suddenly no confusion at all. Teresa will be mother; Louie will do wheelies in the street. One day's oil will burn for eight days, and a Child will be born. And Claire will feel for a long time as she does now—that quite unexpectedly, in spite of everything—she has been lifted into a state of grace.

Setting the Christmas Table

Sally Buckner

Dusk comes early on a Carolina Christmas.
By five, sunlight pales, and shadows stretch
Slender fingers through the greying grass.
Inside, tree lights glisten; on the hearth,
Amber flames beckon cordial greeting.
Counting the plates, I whisper gratitude
For each of the eight who will gather at our
    table
This festive evening. Ted and Serena will
    come
With Dane, Graham, and a steaming casse-
    role.
George will arrive with amoretta coffee
And French bread. Daughter Lynn is already
    here,
Helping prepare, while Bob stokes the fire.
We seem complete.

But, as I reach for the cups,
Something—a flicker of firelight? the scent of
 cider?—
Prompts a reminder of those who will not be
 present.
Their absence aches like an old and stubborn
 wound.

Then Lynn and I unfold Mama's tablecloth—
The one she crocheted on lonely afternoons,
After Daddy died, the silver needle leaping,
Twirling, dipping, within the snowy yarn.
Now her delicate whorl of stars and flowers
Gleams against burnished mahogany.
We set the places; first with Aunt Lella's
 china—
Noritake, made in occupied Japan.
I reach to the highest shelf for Mom B's gob
 lets—
Hobnailed depression glass with a milky glow.
We arrange relishes on the silver tray
Aunt Amy hand-delivered for my wedding;
I can see her now, walking the mile and a half
From the bus station to our house; in one
 hand
A bulging suitcase, in the other the package

She'd wrapped and carried all the way from
   Macon.

Next comes a jar of apricot conserve
Crunchy with cherries; Uncle Jim's recipe.
I make and share it every Christmas season,
And now I spoon it into his berry bowl,
Set it beside the graceful glass pitcher
I inherited from Grandma. Every morning
She'd fill it to the brim with fresh thick cream
From milking done in the dim light of dawn.
Now Lynn brings in dessert: hot-milk cake,
Three cloud-light layers, swirled with silk-
   smooth chocolate,
The recipe from Nina, friend and neighbor.
I close my eyes, remember my first taste.

A rush of car doors, footsteps; I open my eyes.
We're almost ready. Moving around the table,
I brush the cedar tree; ornaments jingle
And a quick aroma springs from prickly
   branches.
I am cast back to childhood afternoons
And Daddy coming home from nearby woods,
Cedar on his shoulder, filling the house
With tangy scent, filling hearts with promise
Of Santa Claus and carols and Mama's fruit-

cake.

Shaking myself back to the present moment,
I find the candles too fat at the base
To fit the silver holders, so I trim them
With Grandpa Stack's bone-handled pocket-
        knife.
I place it on the shelf that Bob constructed
Of lumber salvaged from Grandpa Beaver's
        barn.
It hangs beside the sampler from Aunt Edna,
The one which reads, "And God said, Behold,
I have given you every herb-bearing seed
Which is upon the face of all the earth."

A flurry of steps and voices. I light the candles.
We gather gladly around the brimming table.
Tonight there are eight of us—
                        And many more.

Home for Christmas

Kate Dickens Day

"This is going to be worse than a shivaree," said Papa as the Barkers sat at their cozy kitchen table one brisk morning in early December. Nate had just returned from the post office with a letter from Dan, announcing that he was bringing his English bride, Sheila, to Tarpley for Christmas. He wrote that he wanted Sheila to see where he had grown up and he hoped that other members of the family could come for dinner so they could have a sort of "get acquainted" reunion.

Only that morning Mama had been thinking of the kind of Christmas they would have that year. Since the children were so widely scattered she wouldn't have to worry about a large meal—she could just make dressing for one of Papa's hens, and the home folks could enjoy a quiet, uneventful day. Somehow the idea especially appealed to Mama. "I must be getting old," she thought.

It seemed so short a time to her since all the eight children were under one roof, but now only Mary, the librarian, and Nate, the retired school teacher, were with them. She saw Susan and her family almost daily since they lived so near, but Bob and his five children lived in Oklahoma and Millie, with her husband and step-daughter, lived in Tennessee. Jane and Boyd were still in North Carolina, but their daughter had married an Army officer and was living in Montana and their son was stationed in Washington. Mama's eyes misted over when she counted Janice. The ache, she knew, would always be there. That left only Dan, who had decided to settle in England.

Even before Mary had finished reading Dan's letter, Mama had given up her thoughts for a quiet Christmas and was making plans around the biggest turkey she could find. Of course, they must tell Dan that they would try to do as he wished, and at once they began to count the number of guests they might have. Mary, who liked to tease Papa, said,

"At least, Nate and I won't be adding any more family members to the crowd. Aren't you glad we are both old maids!"

"With thirty people in the family we'll have all we need," said Papa. "If they all do come it will be a once-in-a-lifetime affair and I hope we can survive it."

"And I hope, Mary," said Mama, "that you don't start off with any wild ideas about turning out the whole house from cellar to attic to get ready for them. With that many people here nobody is apt to notice what the house looks like, and as for the cleaning, we'll need to do that after they've come and gone."

Although Christmas was four weeks away both Mary and Mama knew they would go all out to try to make this holiday special, so they began planning furiously for the homecoming. There were menus to concoct, sleeping arrangements to be worked out, yule decorations to be made and hung. The dining table with its extensions would seat twelve people and the kitchen table would accommodate eight, but that made only twenty places. This problem was solved when a friend of Mary's offered a folding table which would seat eight, and since two of the guests were infants who could only use high chairs, that made a place for everyone to sit down at the beginning of the meal. Susan would help with the baking and bring dishes and cutlery over to "fill in the gaps," as Mama said.

They began to hear from the children. Bob and Lula with all of their five children, the daughter-in-law and the grandson would come; Pete, Millie, and Nelly would be with them for the weekend; Boyd and Jane wrote that they would drive up for the day only, bringing Janet and her baby; Stan would fly down from Washington for the day also, and Dan and Sheila planned to arrive on Christmas Eve.

"Oh, I do wish Janet's husband could come," said Mary. "If only he could be here that would make it one hundred percent— every last member of the family under one roof at the same time!"

"No, it wouldn't," said Mama. "Janice is missing."

A week before Christmas Susan's boys brought from the farm bunches of holly and mistletoe along with a beautifully shaped six foot native cedar tree which was placed in front of the big windows in the living room. Long strings of popcorn were looped around it and star-shaped cookies decorated the tips of branches, but the new and special feature for the Barkers was the colored lights which Jane had sent them. Years ago Papa had turned thumbs down on real candles for the tree because of the risk of fire, so the electric bulbs were especially welcomed. On the mantel they arranged one of the ceramic manger scenes that Mary had made for each of the households the year before.

Bob and his family arrived in two cars just before dusk on Christmas Eve, followed soon after by Pete, Millie, and Nelly. Dan and Sheila called that they were spending the night in Asheville and would see them before noon the following day. Counting the homefolks, that made sixteen people to be housed for the night. Mary was intent on placing a certain number in each of the four upstairs bedrooms, but some of the young folks brought their sleeping bags and scattered themselves all through the house.

Christmas morning dawned clear and

cold, but since it was dry underfoot outdoor activities were in full swing. Who wanted to sleep on an occasion such as this? The old tennis court on the south side of the house was soon in action, while some of the youngsters wanted to climb Hamburg mountain and Greg was prevailed upon to go as guide. Dan and Sheila wanted to look over the town and surrounding landscape and Boyd, Stan and Janet went with them. In the kitchen that left Mama, Mary, Susan, Jane and Lula, as Susan said, "to feed Coxey's Army."

They were busy every minute but by their working together they were getting results. Now it seemed they would be ready to serve at the appointed time, shortly after noon. Papa basted the turkey and when it was golden brown he carved it and served it on three platters. There were three baskets of homemade rolls and also three platters of ham. Each table had its own serving dishes, its own vegetables, its own salad, pickle and relishes. Mary decided this would be a good plan to allow everybody to sit at the table at one time and eliminate a lot of fetching and carrying.

Dan came into the kitchen a few minutes before the meal started and drew Mama aside. "Mama, you know Sheila is English and I'm sure that on special occasions she would expect to have wine served with the meal. Do you think Papa would object if we had a little wine, especially for the toasts?"

"I think you already know what the answer will be, Danny, for you know how adamant your father is. When he has once convinced himself that a thing is right or wrong, nothing can change him. Don't you remember when Nate and Mary wanted to play bridge? Papa said they could play Rook, Flinch, Dominoes, Authors, Checkers—anything—but a game with a pack of cards that had a king, queen, and jack in them could never come in his house!" She stirred the rice vigorously for emphasis.

"I really don't think Sheila would mind," she went on. "She seems quite sensible and down-to-earth to me and you could tell her we mountaineers are a pretty independent lot of folks and 'set' in our ways. I have some good grape juice already cold and some blackberry acid—the kind you used to like— and I think we can have our toasts with either of these just as well."

"Okay, old lady, you win," said Dan with a

grin.

When they were all seated and Papa had returned thanks, the toasts were drunk. Little one-year-old Nancy was given Dan's pewter baby cup to drink from. Expecting anything she drank to be milk, she took a sip of the juice, made a wry face and immediately turned the cup upside down on the tray of the high chair. Janet rushed up with a towel to mop up the grape juice, and then she washed Dan's old pewter mug, this time filling it with milk.

This little incident seemed to bring to mind a train of childhood reminiscences. Mary said, "Nate, do you remember the time you got baptized at the table with buttermilk?" To the rest of the listeners she explained, "The minister was having dinner with us that Sunday and it so happened he had christened a child at the morning service. Nate, Jane, Bob and I all sat on a long bench on one side of the table, and as children were taught back then, we sat at the table until the adults were ready to leave. Jane was getting restless so she took up her glass of milk, leaned over Nate and said, 'I baptize you in the name of the father and the son and here you go!' And so saying she emptied the contents of her glass on Nate's head."

"Was that the end of the story?" asked Pete.

"Well, at least it was the end of the dinner party!"

"Susan, you tell about the time you and Millie got into the ants' nest," said Jane.

"Not me," Susan replied, "if it is told let Millie do the telling."

That story was told, and another and another. The ones who had heard them before seemed to enjoy them more than ever. Eventually Boyd looked at his watch. "My friends," he said, "as pleasant as this is, we poor folks who have to work tomorrow need to be getting on with the tree and then starting our trip back home."

They trooped into the living room, the first to arrive taking possession of all the chairs and couches and the overflow sitting in a semicircle on the floor opposite the tree. Greg had agreed to act as Santa Claus and Susan had fixed a costume for him. He said he'd wear the suit, pillow front and all, but he drew the line at putting on the beard. In thirty minutes Santa with some helpers had stripped the tree and removed the stacks of packages from the floor around it. Everyone tore open the packages the minute they were received, and as the happy recipients shouted thanks to pleased donors the room became noisier and noisier. When things had calmed down a bit Mary said, "I know we can't spend much more time, but let's have a song or two before you leave."

With Dan and his banjo and Pete with his guitar, they all stood knee deep in wrapping paper and sang "Silent Night" and "Joy to the World." After a few more carols they caught hands for a lusty rendition of "Auld Lang Syne."

The days following were a sort of kaleidoscope to Mama and Mary. They got through with one meal and by the time the washing up for it was finished, the next repast had to be underway. Friends and relatives dropped in to see the ones still visiting. In two days after Christmas the fruit cake was almost gone and Mary was in the kitchen frantically stirring up another one to insure there being something to serve callers with their afternoon coffee or tea.

At last, on Saturday morning, the visitors began their trek back home. The house itself resembled a bee hive as families tried to collect their belongings, pack their bags, and stow them in the cars. "Why is it," asked Betty to no one in particular, "that when you get ready to go on a trip, all your clothes will fit nicely into a suitcase, but when you start home a week later, those very same clothes won't go back in that very same case?"

"I can't tell you why, but I can vouch for what you are saying," said Bob, Jr. "It happens to me every time I go anywhere."

By midmorning everybody was on his way and Papa celebrated by going back to bed for another nap. Mama was busy collecting the mountain of sheets and pillow cases she would have to wash, gathering up the discarded Christmas wrappings, taking down the tree which was beginning to shed, when all of a sudden a paralyzing weariness overcame her and she sat down in an easy chair. She thought she would rest a bit before going on with her chores. It was sweet to sit still and know that she didn't have to hurry—it was ever so good to be alone and to sit there not even thinking.

Papa wakened from his nap, took a walk around the grounds, sawed a little wood and stacked it in the shed joining the back porch, and then walked up to the mail box to get the evening paper. In the meantime Mary had come back from a trip to town and had gone to the kitchen to see about supper. When they were ready to eat and Mama still had not stirred, Papa went in to see about her. "Cora," he said and shook her gently.

Mama opened her eyes, stared blindly ahead of her for a few seconds and then asked foolishly, "Have I been asleep?"

When they had finished eating they still sat in the cozy corner of the kitchen, unwinding and living over the events of the last week. Mary was happy with the reunion and said so with enthusiasm. Papa said it was fine, of course, but something you couldn't repeat many times in a lifetime. Mama said she was like old Uncle Billy Bradford, who when he was describing the departure of some lingering house guests said: "When I saw the last car go down the driveway—them was the purtiest tail lights I ever did see!"

Firecrackers at Christmas

Robert Morgan

In the Southern mountains, our big
serenade was not the Fourth but
always Christmas Eve and Christmas.
Starting at midnight the valleys
and branch coves fairly shook with barks
of crackers, boom of shotguns, jolt
even of sticks of dynamite.
You would have thought a new hunting
season had begun in the big-star
night, or that a war had broken
out in the scattered hollows: all
the feuds and land disputes come to
a magnum finale. The sparks
everywhere of match and fuse
and burst were like giant lightning bugs.
Thunder doomed the ridges though
the sky shone clear and frost sugared

the meadows. Yankees were astonished
at the violence and racket
on the sacred day, they said, as
cherrybombs were hurled into yards
and placed expanding mailboxes
same as Halloween. Perhaps the custom
had its origins in peasant-pagan
times of honoring the solstice
around a burning tree, or in
the mystery centuries of
saluting the miraculous
with loudest brag and syllable.
Certainly the pioneer had
no more valuable gift to bring
than lead and powder to offer
in the hush of hills, the long rifles
their best tongues for saying the peace
they claimed to carry to the still
unchapeled wilderness, just as
cannon had been lit in the Old
World to announce the birth of kings.
They fired into the virgin skies
a ceremony we repeated
ignorantly. But what delight
I felt listening in the unheated
bedroom dark, not believing in
Santa Claus or expensive gifts,

to the terrible cracks along
the creek road and up on Olivet,
as though great rivers of ice were
breaking on the horizon and
trees were bursting at the heart
and new elements were being born
in whip-stings and distant booms
and the toy chatter of the littlest
powder grace notes. That was our
roughest and best caroling.

Biographies

Ellyn Bache has published three novels, *Safe Passage* which was made into a movie starring Susan Sarandon and Sam Shepard, *Festival in Fire Season* and most recently *The Activist's Daughter*. Her collection of short stories, *The Value of Kindness*, won the Willa Cather Fiction Prize. She lives in Wilmington.

Joseph Bathanti came to North Carolina as a VISTA Volunteer in 1976 and now lives in Statesville where he is a member of the English Faculty at Mitchell Community College. Bathanti is the author of four books of poetry. He has been the recipient of a North Carolina Literary Fellowship and the Sam Ragan Award.

Sue Ellen Bridgers grew up in Winterville, in Pitt County, and now lives in Sylva. Her young-adult novels have won several awards.

Sally Buckner has published articles, poems, fiction and plays. She is a professor of English at Peace College.

175

Kathryn Stripling Byer is poet in residence at Western Carolina University. Her second collection, *Wildwood Flower*, won the Lamont Poetry Selection from the Academy of American Poets.

Irene Cheshire has worked as a deputy clerk in the Wake County courts and as director at WPTF Radio. She lives in Raleigh.

Michael Chitwood's poetry and fiction have appeared in *Poetry*, *The Southern Review* and *Threepenny Review*. He has three published books of poetry—*Salt Works*, *Whet* and *The Weave Room*.

Shirley Cochrane teaches creative writing at American University. She has published two collections of poetry, and a novel, *Everything That is All*.

Kate Pickens Day, born in Weaverville in 1894, kept the books for her husband's lumber business and wrote a weekly newspaper column. At eighty-six, eye sight failing and bed-ridden, she wrote in long hand a novel, *Only When They're Little* that was published by Appalachian Consortium Press. She died in 1984.

Kaye Gibbons published her first novel, *Ellen Foster*, when she was twenty-six. She has received the Sue Kaufman Award from the American Academy and Institute of Arts and Letters, a National Endowment for the Arts Fellowship, a PEN/Revson Award, a Citation from the Ernest Hemingway Foundation, the Chicago Tribune's Heartland Prize and other honors. She lives in Raleigh.

Marianne Gingher is the author of a novel, *Bobby Rex's Greatest Hits*, which received North Carolina's Sir Walter Raleigh Award, and a collection of short stories, *Teen Angel*. She directs the creative writing program at the University of North Carolina at Chapel Hill.

Robert Inman, a former anchorman for WBTV News in Charlotte, has published three novels, *Home Fires Burning*, which was made into a Hallmark Hall of Fame presentation, *Old Dogs and Children* and most recently, *Dairy Queen Days*. Inman has written and had produced five other television scripts.

Julian Mason has published two books, *The Poems of Phillis Wheatley* and *Search Party*. He lives in Charlotte.

Rebecca McClanahan has published three collections of poetry and worked for fifteen years as poet-in-residence for the Charlotte Mecklenburg Schools.

Michael McFee was born in Asheville and graduated from the University of North Carolina at Chapel Hill where he is currently on the English Faculty. He has lived in Durham since l979 and published five collections of poetry. Most recently McFee won the Five Points Poetry Prize.

Lenard D. Moore won the Haiku Museum of Tokyo Award in l983 and 1994. He is Founder and Executive Director of the Carolina African American Writers' Collective and author of *Desert Storm: A Brief History* and

Forever Home. He lives in Raleigh.

Ruth Moose has published two collections of short stories and four books of poetry including *Making the Bed*, which won the Oscar Arnold Young Award from the Poetry Society of North Carolina. Moose has had three PEN Awards for short story, and teaches writing at the University of North Carolina. She lives in Albemarle and Chapel Hill.

Robert Morgan teaches at Cornell University. He has published seven collections of poetry, received a Guggenheim Award, four NEA fellowships and the North Carolina Award for Literature.

Sam Ragan, who died in 1996, was the poet laureate of North Carolina. He was editor and publisher of *The Pilot* in Southern Pines and served as the first Secretary of the North Carolina Department of Cultural Resources.

Jean Rodenbough is Staff Chaplain at Morehead Memorial Hospital in Eden. She lives in Madison with her husband Charlie. They have four grown children and seven grandchildren.

Bland Simpson is the author of *Heart of the County*, *The Great Dismal* and *The Mystery of Beautiful Nell Cropsey*. A member of the internationally acclaimed string band, The Red Clay Ramblers, he has collaborated on such musicals as "Diamond Studs," "Fool Moon" and "Kudzu."

Lee Smith is the author of two collections of short stories and nine novels, including *Fair and Tender Ladies* and *Saving Grace*. The recipient of many prizes and awards, her most recent include a Lyndhurst grant and a three-year Lila Wallace-Reader's Digest Writer's Award. She lives in Hillsborough.

Stephen Smith has taught at Sandhills Community College in Southern Pines since l97l. He is editor of *Sandhills Review*.

Shelby Stephenson's poems have appeared in *The Hudson Review*, *Ohio Review* and *Poetry Northwest*. Since l979, he has been editor of *Pembroke Magazine*. He teaches at UNC-Pembroke and lives with his wife Linda in Benson on the farm where he was born.

About the Illustrator:
Talmadge Moose received his BFA from Virginia Commonwealth University. He is listed in *Who's Who in Art* and the *International Directory of Art*.